THE CAMINO DIARIES

DOUG McPHILLIPS

Also, by Doug McPhillips:
Other Visionary Stories:
NOVELS.
From Darkness to Light.
Awake to my Gutted Dream.
The Sword of Discernment.
Santiago Traveller.
I Prophet.
Master's at my table.
The Guru of Jerusalem.
We are upside down. (Biography)
The Wicklow Way.
The Adventures of Ace McDice.
Instant Karma & Grace.
The Credo.
Reflections of an Old Man.
Reincarnation of the Assassin
Master of The Arts
Masters of Introspection.
King of the O' Malley
Journey to a hermit's haven.
The Rise and Rise of a 4th Reich
Grandad's tales are tall and true.
Into Action: Alcoholics for Jesus
Lightbulb Moments
For Pete's Sake
Walking in my Shadow
A Pilgrim's Last Hurrah
The Legends of Merlin
Sweet Surrender
Camino Guide Book.

Country Camino. (Album).
Santiago Traveller. (Album).
Soul Fact. (Album).

Doug McPhillips Circa 2025: ISBN 978-1-7645804-6-1

National Library of Australia Catalogue-in-Publication data:
New Holy Bible, International Version, Hodder & Stoughton, 1980. Alcoholics Anonymous, 4th Edition, AA World Service, 1976.
Daily Reflections, 11th Print, AA World Service 2014.
Journey to the Inner Mountain, Hodder & Staughton, James Cowan, 2002.
The Choice is always ours, Jove Publishing, 1997.
Sword of Discernment, IngramSpark, Doug McPhillips, 2015
Santiago traveller, Ingram Spark, Doug McPhillips, 2018.
Wicklow Way, Ingram Spark, Doug McPhillips, 2018.
Notebook Research.
Google research- Authors Unknown.

This book blends fact and fiction. All characters in this novel are either factual or fictional, and the names of people living at the time may be real or imagined. Any resemblance to actual events, locales, or persons, living or dead, is purely coincidental; however, what is applicable is indeed real. Where poetic license transforms fact into fiction, names have been altered to protect the innocent.

"A pilgrimage is a journey, not to find new places, but to discover profound truths as we walk towards what matters."

- Doug McPhillips

For those who are among the noblest of men
And the least of God's servants.

Introduction

This book is a reflection on the many pilgrimages I have undertaken in search of a deeper meaning in life. My journey began more than a decade before I embarked on my first official pilgrimage. It didn't arise from grand expectations but rather from the weight of multiple tragedies that accumulated in a single year—a year filled with pain, loss, and suffering that compelled me to seek escape. I sought solace in alcohol and fleeting relationships, but these only brought more sorrow, remorse, and a more profound sense of disillusionment. Yet, through this unravelling, the path revealed itself, guiding me along the long road of pilgrimage and ultimately leading me to discover myself.

It was by chance that I finally decided to walk the Camino, and in me something shifted. There, along the ancient paths trodden by countless souls before me, I kept my first true daily diary. Each day I wrote — not just where I walked, but what within me as I walked. The rhythm of the road opened me, invited me, healed me. Journaling became as essential as the walking itself.

That habit travelled with me on every pilgrimage I undertook in the years that followed — across countries, across seasons of life, across inner landscapes I had long avoided. My diaries became companions on the trail, silent witnesses to transformation.

Now, as I dust off these old notebooks — weathered, creased, and full of the sweat and breath of the journey — I recognise the story they hold. This book is shaped from those pages: part memory, part reflection, part rediscovery. It looks back with interest, forward with wonder, and inward with honesty.

I share these writings not as a teacher, nor as someone who has mastered the spiritual path, but as a fellow traveller — a pilgrim learning still. I hope that within these reflections, you may find echoes of your own journey. Whether you walk the Camino or the quiet roads of daily life, pilgrimage is less about distance and more about willingness: the willingness to face ourselves, to surrender what no longer serves us, and to open to what the journey offers.

May these pages accompany you as you walk your own way — with curiosity, courage, and a heart ready to be surprised.

Chapter 1. Stepping Stones

Dusting off my old diary entries—those scattered reflections gathered over a decade of walking the Camino—I am reminded that pilgrimage was a habit long before I ever knew the word. As a small boy, whenever melancholy settled over me, or the ache of abandonment pressed too close, I would set out in search of answers. Feeling alone in the world, I walked. Sometimes it was a bush track leading me into the quiet company of trees and sky; other times, a lone walk along a peaceful beach, watching the waves roll in like long wake trails to the shore, listening to the steady roar of the ocean. Even then, without realising it, I was learning to meet my inner storms with movement, mystery, and the healing presence of nature.

Memories float back now as I write—those halcyon days of childhood adventure, when I lived out the dreams of my imagination and relished every moment spent in the bush with friends. We hunted for colourful birds' eggs to add to our collections, or roamed like wild youths with slingshots, sometimes taking the life of a bird or the occasional lizard for the sheer thrill of it. It was our own untamed garden of Eden, where innocence and mischief intertwined, and where the world felt boundless, mysterious, and ours to explore.

There were also the days spent with our Aboriginal schoolmates, who seemed more naturally attuned to the rhythms of the land than we ever were. They could catch fish with ease, spearing them with a sharpened stick or crafting a woomera. This ingenious handheld tool added leverage, speed, and accuracy to a thrown spear, usually aimed at an animal that could feed a family, like a kangaroo or a rabbit. We learned so much from these friends—far more, it seemed, than from our early lessons in religious instruction or the basics of reading, writing, and arithmetic. Life felt freer back then than it does for children today. After school, our days were filled with sport, exploration, and simple fun in the bush, as long as we were home by dark. On weekends, once our chores were done and any schoolwork finished, we were free to roam from daylight until dusk, answering only to the pull of curiosity and the call of the wild.

As the years passed and childhood gave way to adolescence, the bush tracks and beaches of my youth slowly turned into pathways of inner questioning. The carefree adventures of earlier days began to mingle with a growing awareness of myself and the world around me. The loneliness that had once driven me out the door with childish curiosity became something I tried to understand more consciously. I didn't have the language for it then, but looking back, those wanderings were the first stirrings of a lifelong search for belonging and meaning.

While my friends grew absorbed in sport, schoolyard rivalries, and the first signs of youthful independence, I often found myself slipping away to quiet places. A river bend. A hilltop. A patch of scrub no one else bothered with. These became my sanctuaries—little hermitages where my young heart tried to make sense of life's early wounds. I walked because the act of walking soothed something wordless inside me. I watched the flight of birds, the shifting clouds, the slow turning of the day, and in these simple rhythms I found a peace I could find nowhere else.

At school, we were taught the doctrines of faith—Scripture, catechism, the stories of saints and martyrs. Yet I sensed, even then, that there was another kind of knowing, one that could not be learned from a chalkboard or recited from memory. It lived in silence, in observation, in the feeling of wind on the face or the scent of rain on dry earth.

My early wanderings had already shown me that God—though I did not think of the divine in such formal terms—was as present in the natural world as in any sermon. By the time I entered my teenage years, I had begun to carry this inner world quietly with me, often unnoticed by others. Friends saw only the boy who joined in their games, shared their laughter, and followed the expected rhythms of growing up. But beneath the surface, the old ache of abandonment still whispered in quiet hours. The longing to understand myself—to make sense of the absence I felt—kept me walking, searching, dreaming of distant horizons.

It would take many years, and many more paths, before I understood that these early wanderings were preparing me for something larger. They were rehearsals for the pilgrim life that would one day call me across oceans and continents, onto the ancient roads of the Camino. But even then, in the raw and restless years of youth, I was already learning what every pilgrim eventually discovers: that the journey inward begins long before the journey outward, and that the footsteps of childhood often echo into adulthood in ways we only recognise much later.

Early adulthood arrived not with clarity, but with a restless pull—an inner stirring that told me life was calling me forward, even if I did not yet know in which direction. Like many young men of my generation, I stepped into the world eager for independence yet burdened with questions I carried quietly, questions about belonging, love, purpose, and the shadows that lingered from childhood. I tried to convince myself that ambition, work, or the pursuit of companionship might soften those hidden edges inside me, but the ache for understanding remained.

Relationships in those years were often shaped more by the wounds of my past than by any real wisdom. I longed for connection, sometimes too deeply, hoping that another person might fill the hollow spaces where abandonment had once lived. And when bonds fractured—as they often did—I felt the ripples more sharply than most. Each ending seemed to echo that old childhood loneliness, stirring up memories I thought I had long outgrown. Yet even amid these emotional storms, I kept moving. I worked hard, tried to build a life, and embraced every opportunity that pointed toward growth, even if I didn't always recognise it at the time.

There were moments, however, when the old instinct returned —the call to walk, to step away from the noise of the world and listen once more to the quiet truth beneath it all. I would find myself wandering again, just as I had as a boy… down forgotten bush tracks, along the coastline at dusk, or into the solitude of the countryside. These were not idle walks; they were acts of survival, a way to steady myself when the complexities of adulthood pressed too heavily upon me. In those lonely hours of reflection, nature remained my oldest companion, reminding me that even in uncertainty, a deeper rhythm is at work. In time, I began to sense that the answers I sought would not be found through force or striving. There was a different kind of guidance waiting for me—something ancient, timeless, and patient. A quiet invitation to surrender, to let go of the old stories that bound me, and to trust in a journey yet unseen. At the time, I did not know where it would lead, only that the longing within me had grown into a call I could no longer ignore.

And so, without realising it, the seeds of pilgrimage were already taking root. The boy who wandered for solace, the teenager who walked to understand himself, and the young man who sought healing in movement—all of these selves were slowly forming the pilgrim I would eventually become. The Camino was still far beyond the horizon of my life, but the path toward it had already begun, quietly, faithfully, in the deepest parts of my being.

As adulthood settled more firmly around me, life began to reveal its harsher edges. The trials that had once felt distant or imagined during youth now arrived with full weight: responsibilities, disappointments, heartbreak, and the realisation that no one escapes life without walking through shadows. For me, the deepest challenges were often emotional, shaped by a childhood in which connection felt uncertain, and love could seem conditional. Whenever relationships faltered or trust was shaken, the old scars surfaced, reminding me of how fragile a heart can be when shaped by early wounds.

There came a time when the cumulative strain of these struggles pressed so heavily upon me that I found myself standing at a crossroads. I felt unanchored, stretched between the demands of the world and the quiet truth within me that insisted there had to be more—more meaning, more peace, more understanding of who I truly was beneath the roles I played each day. It wasn't a single event that broke me open, but a series of minor fractures: the unspoken hurts, the pain of loss, the sense of giving more than I received, and the slow erosion of certainty about the life I was trying to build.

In the midst of this turmoil, I found myself returning instinctively to the places of my youth—bush tracks, coastal cliffs, the solitude of nature where the wind carried a language

I felt but could never fully explain. There, away from the expectations of others, I could breathe again. I could feel my own soul stirring, urging me to listen, to pause, to accept that something in my life needed to change. I realised that the outward striving I had pursued for so long had led me further from my inner truth, not closer to it. During this period, I began writing in earnest—poems, fragments of thoughts, half-formed prayers to a God I wasn't sure I believed in but desperately hoped was listening. These writings were raw, unguarded, and deeply personal. They became my companions in the nights when sleep would not come, and my mind replayed old memories like a film I had grown tired of watching. In the quiet moments of putting pen to paper, I felt the beginnings of a shift, as if naming my pain allowed something new to move within me.

It was here, in this inward landscape of struggle and awakening, that the idea of pilgrimage returned—not as a childhood escape, but as a deliberate, soul-led calling. I felt drawn to a journey that demanded surrender, one that would strip away the noise of daily life and lead me, step by step, toward a deeper understanding of myself and the divine presence I sensed just beyond the edges of my awareness.

Little did I know that this longing would soon carry me across the world to the ancient pathways of Spain, where countless pilgrims had walked before me. The Camino had not yet appeared as a clear destination, but the yearning for transformation—the need to heal, to reconcile my past, and to reclaim a sense of purpose—was growing stronger by the day. When the time finally came, I would recognise it not as an escape, but as a return: a return to myself, to that wandering boy who sought answers in nature, and to the quiet voice within that whispered of a way forward.

In the midst of depression and anxiety—when my world had come unstuck and the ways I had lived, driven by worldly desires and illusion, no longer held me up—I stumbled upon the story of St. James. After the death of Christ, James journeyed across Spain, preaching a faith born not of empty words but of action and inner transformation. His mission echoed the message he had received from Jesus Himself: to follow a path not of this world, for *"My kingdom is not of this world."*

That message stirred something in me, a longing for another way. And my thoughts drifted back to the Dreaming of my boyhood—those times with my Aboriginal schoolmates who spoke of their ancestors' spirits, of how the land was formed, and of the sacred relationship between their people and the stars, trees, hills, animals, and all living things. Everything, they said, was shaped in the **Dreamtime,** that realm of spiritual consciousness where meaning and creation intertwine.

Their stories had touched me then, even before I understood why. And now, in my brokenness, they touched me again — whispering that there were older ways, more profound ways, paths walked long before my own stumbling steps.

It was as if two ancient roads—one Christian, one Indigenous —were calling me back to the same truth: that the journey of healing is inward before it is outward, and that the earth beneath our feet remembers far more than we do.

And so the Camino found me—or perhaps, in the way of great spiritual journeys, it had been waiting all along.

It is said that **the Camino—*The Way*,** as pilgrims call it—lies beneath the band of the Milky Way, following ancient ley-lines that mirror the energies flowing from the stars above. In

Eastern philosophy, the spiritual life force (prana) is believed to be inseparably connected to the life-giving power of the sun, and many hold that this force is powerful along energetic pathways that run through our galaxy, other galaxies, and distant star systems. The Camino, aligned with these earthly ley lines, begins in France at Saint-Jean-Pied-de-Port and winds its way east to west over the Pyrenees, across desert plains, through hills and valleys, until it reaches the great cathedral of Santiago de Compostela, where the remains of St. James the Greater are believed to rest beneath the high altar.

At that stage of my life, I was more interested in the journey than the destination. I made a few plans, carried no rigid expectations, and prepared only by downloading a rough guide listing the distances between towns, villages, and cities. I simply looked at the long road ahead and wondered how many days it might take me to walk it—one step after another, trusting that the path itself would teach me what I needed to learn.

And so it was, with an overpacked knapsack, a tent, and a sleeping bag slung awkwardly over my shoulder, that I set out —catching a flight to Paris in the hope of overcoming melancholy and a disgruntled spirit. I had only the faintest idea of how to reach the official starting point of the Camino, and in truth, I had not even consulted a proper map of the route. All I carried was a single sheet of paper listing the distances between the towns and villages ahead.

Looking back, I see that this was my first, unknowing step on the spiritual path of surrender. I had handed myself over to whatever would come, trusting—without yet realising it—that I would be led where I needed to go.

Arriving in Paris, I felt both excited and utterly out of place. The city moved with a rhythm far quicker than my unsettled heart. People hurried with purpose, knowing exactly where they were going, while I wandered through the airport terminals with no real plan except to somehow make my way toward the Pyrenees.

Yet beneath the confusion, something quiet stirred—an awareness that I had stepped onto unfamiliar ground not only in a foreign country, but within myself. The weight of my knapsack pressed into my shoulders, and with every step, I felt the heaviness of the life I had left behind.

The bus traffic into the city became a little frustrating, so I got impatient, left the bus, and found my way to the Metro, changing trains where needed, and alighted a couple of streets short of the Hotel "Welcome" on the Rue de Seine, where I had booked to stay. I was feeling proud that I had mastered the transport system in one fell swoop and was thinking I was pretty clever.

So it was that I entered the Welcome hotel with some false pride, which often comes before a fall. And that is what happened: coming out of the sunlight into the dark entry of the hotel, I tripped on a small lip of a step at the entry and fell face-first onto the tiled floor, breaking my sunglasses and cutting my nose, cracking my head on the impact. The concierge came quickly to my aid, and it was not long before I was led to my room, showered, and dressed in fresh clothing before falling asleep for a short spell. I awoke with a headache and saw the two black eyes staring back at me in the mirror.

In the quiet of that Paris hotel room, as I studied the bruised face staring back at me from the mirror, something stirred deep within. The fall had been sudden, humiliating, and painful—but it also carried a message. Not a message heard with the ears, but one felt in the soul. I had come to Europe burdened with sorrow, pride, confusion, and the remnants of a life that had unravelled. I thought I was stepping onto the Camino as a pilgrim seeking answers. But the fall reminded me that I was not yet humbled enough to receive them.

Chapter 2- The Way Ahead.

It struck me that the Camino had begun its teachings before I had even reached the mountains. The Way was telling me, *"Leave your pride at the door."* Literally, I had tripped on the threshold—on the very point between the life I had known and the unknown path ahead.

The bruises became symbols of something far more profound:
– a breaking down of old habits, – a softening of the ego,
– a surrender to forces greater than my own will.

In many spiritual traditions, the first step of an actual journey is a fall, a collapse of certainty that opens the heart to transformation. As I sat with the ache in my head and the sting on my nose, I realised that this fall had not been an accident— it was an initiation. The Way had humbled me so it could teach me. It had wounded me so that I might heal. It had stopped me so that I might finally begin. And so the Camino's first lesson came not through prayer, or meditation, or the steady rhythm of walking, but through the shock of striking the earth—the same earth I would soon walk across for hundreds of kilometres.

It had been my habit since my time in rehabilitation recovering from depression, anxiety and the aftermath of having given up drinking alcohol excessively, that I took to writing a daily diary and recording any poetic thoughts that came to mind. It was the same diary that I now refer to, recalling the words I recorded. My Camino de Santiago didn't start at the base of the Pyrenees mountains; it began in Paris, on that first Camino.
I was feeling unwell from my fall as I boarded the train, lifting my backpack, tent, and sleeping bag onto the rack above my head. Almost as an afterthought, I reached in and pulled out

my diary and a pen—hoping that writing might distract me from the throbbing headache and the unsettled feeling in my stomach.

What happened on that train journey became the catalyst for a future I could never have imagined. As the countryside blurred past the window, I began to write a poem about my grandfather. The words came slowly at first, then with a sudden, surprising clarity. I had no idea then that this simple poem, written to ease the pain of a fall, would eventually transform into a song recorded by an international folk-rock musician. Nor could I have known that this moment would mark the quiet beginning of my life as a writer of songs and novels. Of course, none of that was visible to me then. I was focused only on my journey of recovery, seeking the inner truth of my spiritual descent and the healing I desperately needed. Ahead of me lay many highs and lows of steps along The Way. Yet on that train, the first threads of my future were already being woven. I had come to walk the Camino—but the Camino had already begun walking in me.

Diary Entry – Sunday, 21 July 2013
Saint-Jean-Pied-de-Port

Changed trains at Bayonne today—my final stretch toward Saint-Jean. I arrived early in the evening to the unexpected sound of trumpets and drums, and to a village alive with celebration. Only later did I learn it was the town's hundredth anniversary. The entire population seemed to be dressed in period costume, filling the narrow streets with laughter, colour, and the rhythm of old traditions brought to life again.
The summer sun was still high, casting a warm glow over everything as I threaded my way through the crowded streets. I felt both a stranger and somehow welcomed by the energy of it all.

I made my way to the Hotel Itzalpea—thank God I had booked it months earlier. That small act of planning, the only real preparation I had done for the Camino, turned out to be a blessing. Every room in the village was taken for the celebrations. It seems The Way provides even when we don't realise we're being guided.

A local woman pointed me toward the hotel, and after confirming my booking with the keeper, I climbed the steep spiral staircase to my room in the third-floor attic. Small, clean, and simple—just right for a pilgrim. The window looked out over a patchwork of red terracotta rooftops, and beyond them, the dark shape of the Pyrenees rose against the evening sky. I stood there for a while, letting the view settle inside me. Those mountains—silent, ancient, and waiting— would be my first challenge tomorrow. [For now, I am grateful for this tiny attic room, this unexpected celebration, and the feeling that something in my life is beginning to shift, step by step, even before I take my first one on The Way.]

The mountains were silhouetted now as the sun slipped behind the horizon, yet the heat lingered—still close to forty degrees even at 8 p.m. I recall as I put down the diary I had been reading from and remembered that I took my time under a cool shower, letting the water ease the ache in my head and the tension in my body. After a short rest, I dressed and wandered out in search of a meal.

I chose a small restaurant with outdoor tables and ordered a soft drink—my commitment to leave alcohol behind was still firm within me. As I ate, the last echoes of the day's festival drifted through the streets, the drums fading into the distance. Across from me stood a great fort-like wall, its red-brick houses framed by white concrete. Something about that scene stayed with me. I sensed I would see this blend of stone, colour, and history repeated throughout the Basque Country I would soon walk through.

Just as I was finishing my meal, a final parade appeared—a line of horse-drawn carts with small boys guiding the reins, their faces lit with a mixture of pride and playfulness. Behind them came a cluster of carriages, again led by children dressed in period costume. The procession ended with young drummers tapping slow, steady rhythms on kettle drums, the sound rolling across the twilight and up into the foothills of the mountains beyond.

I tore off the last piece of bread from the plate and savoured the quiet that followed. Then I returned to my attic room above the red terracotta rooftops, pausing to take one final photograph of the fading light over the village.

As I lay on my bed, the shadowy outline of the Pyrenees filled the open window. Those dark, ancient forms seemed to call to me—a silent invitation to step into something deeper, something long awaited. Tomorrow, my Camino will begin. And with it, a spiritual awakening I could sense but not yet understand.

Diary Entry – Monday Morning, 22 July 2013
Saint-Jean-Pied-de-Port

As I stirred awake today, my thoughts wandered back to the parade from last night—the small children guiding horses and carriages with such confidence, no older than eight or nine. I realise now that those same children would be young adults in their early twenties today. How time races on.

I couldn't help but wonder what paths they've taken—whether they've grown into their lives with grace or stumbled as I once did. It took me decades to settle into myself. In my twenties, I was wild, reckless, living dangerously, as though the world was infinite and consequences were for others. Perhaps these reflections are simply the Camino preparing me to look gently at my own past.

My mind drifted then to the entries I had written in my old diary, and I returned to the moment of waking this morning. I rose to the hot morning sun streaming into my attic refuge. It was around 8:30 a.m.—the latest I had slept since arriving in Europe three weeks earlier. Another shower to shake off the heat, then I repacked my backpack with the familiar mix of excitement and uncertainty that comes before a journey.

Descending the spiral staircase, I was greeted by the smell of a hearty breakfast. The innkeeper pointed to a thermometer already reading 40 degrees Celsius. A tough day ahead, I thought. I paid my bill, filled both water bottles from the jug on the breakfast table, and tucked a bundle of bread rolls into my pack. In my haste to get started on The Way, I forgot to properly check the attic room. Only later did I realise I had left my phone charger plugged into the wall socket, a minor oversight that would follow me for days. I found myself borrowing chargers from kind pilgrims along The Way until I eventually located a shop with a replacement. Still, such inconveniences are part of the Camino's lessons—gentle reminders to slow down, be present, and accept both the mishaps and the unexpected help that arrive when needed.

Stepping out from the cool shade of the hotel doorway into the already blistering heat, I felt a strange mixture of excitement and vulnerability. The village was just beginning to stir— shopkeepers raising shutters, a few pilgrims tightening straps on their packs, the scent of fresh bread drifting through the narrow streets.

I made my way toward the old **Pilgrims' Gate, the Porte Saint-Jacques,** stopping for a moment beneath its ancient stones. Countless pilgrims had passed through this very arch before me—some desperate, some hopeful, some searching, others simply curious. Today, I was all of these at once.

The climb began almost immediately towards **Orisson**, some eight kilometres away and 1450 metres above me. The road wound sharply upward, leading away from the village and into the open fields that leaned toward the mountains. The heat pressed down even though it was still early. Sweat trickled down my back within minutes, the weight of my overpacked backpack making each step heavier than I had imagined.

An omen at the base of the first marker—a dead asp!

"Snakes and Arrows cannot go where sound remains forever." There it lay, a rather large snake curled neatly as though placed there on purpose, like some ancient warning to all who dared step onto the trail—a reminder of the dangers that might wait among the rocky outcrops and tall, waving grasses ahead.

Snakes were the last thing I had expected on the Camino. Australia is full of them—every second bushwalk carries the possibility of crossing paths with something venomous—but here, in the Pyrenees? I had never given it a thought. Yet there it was, my first Camino companion: stone, sunlight, and a lifeless serpent at my feet. Was it a sign? Or simply nature doing what nature does? Either way, it sharpened my senses. My pilgrimage had begun.

I took a slow breath and stepped around the snake, adjusting the straps of my pack as though preparing for something greater than a simple day's walk. Ahead of me, the path began to rise, first gently, then with the steady insistence of a mountain that does not negotiate. The morning heat was already gathering, pressing against my back as I took my first real steps toward Orisson.

The air smelled of dew and dust and distant pasture. Bells from grazing animals drifted faintly across the valley, and now and then a pilgrim's voice echoed somewhere behind me, carried forward on the hot breeze. My legs, still stiff from the fall days earlier, protested the incline, but there was a strange determination in me—almost a stubbornness I hadn't expected.

With each step, the world grew quieter. The small town I had left behind fell away, replaced by the rhythm of my breathing, the crunch of gravel, the pulse of my own thoughts. I was no longer the man on a train nursing a headache, scribbling lines about his grandfather. I was becoming something else—a traveller stepping into uncertainty, not yet aware that this mountain, this day, and this path would shape the decade ahead.

The climb grew steeper as the morning advanced, the heat settling over the mountains like a heavy cloak. My shirt clung to my back, and the straps of my pack dug into my shoulders with an insistence that made me pause more often than I cared to admit. The thought of jettisoning my tent and sundry other items crossed my mind, but I at this point, I may need them all. By mid-morning, the sun was merciless, and the water I'd filled that morning was disappearing far quicker than I anticipated.

I stopped in the shade of a lone tree, lifted my bottle, and felt the weight of it—light, too light. Only a few mouthfuls remained. A flicker of worry shook me. Forty degrees at sea level was one thing; forty degrees on a steep climb in the **Pyrenees** was something else entirely.

The road to Orisson stretched before me like a promise and a test. And a test it proved to be, for it was not long before I ran out of water and as luck would have it, I soon reached the 1450 viewpoint. Not long after, I came upon a young pilgrim sitting on a rock, his face flushed and tired. He held his empty bottle upside down as if hoping a stray drop might appear.

"Run dry?" I asked.

He gave a half-laugh, half-groan. "Completely. You?"

" Yeah, me too."

There was a moment of shared understanding—two strangers united by the simple, primal need for water. We decided to keep walking together, encouraging each other through the climb. Our steps were slow, measured, and deliberate. The heat shimmered off the path, making the distant slopes waver like a mirage.

Then, as if placed there by mercy itself, we spotted a large metal water tank beside a stone fence—clearly meant for livestock. We approached it sceptically, unsure if it would offer anything fit for human use. But just beside the tank, half-hidden by overgrown grass and a cluster of thistles, was a slight metal tap fixed to a pipe. The young pilgrim turned it.

A single drip fell. Then another. Then a steady, clear stream.

We laughed—real, relieved laughter that carried across the hillside. We rinsed our faces, soaked our hats, and drank greedily until our bellies were full and we had recovered enough to continue our journey.

By the time we reached Orisson, the heat of the day seemed to ease its grip, replaced by a gentle breeze drifting down from the higher ridges. The small cluster of buildings—little more than a refuge, a terrace, and a scattering of outbuildings—felt like an oasis balanced precariously on the mountainside. Pilgrims rested in pockets of shade, boots off, shirts draped across railings to dry. There was a sense of camaraderie in the air, the kind that comes only from shared struggle.

I found a seat on the terrace overlooking the valley below, ordered a cool drink, and took out my diary. The simple act of putting pen to paper steadied me. I wrote slowly, letting the events of the morning settle into place—the heat, the dead asp at the milestone, the long climb, the moment of panic when my water ran low, and the minor miracle of the hidden tap and meeting a fellow pilgrim of The Way in a similar predicament.

This habit of journaling, once sporadic and uncertain, had by now become a quiet ritual—one I would return to every evening throughout my Camino journeys. I didn't know then just how precious these notes would become, or how they would later shape the bones of my story, my novel, my reflections on the Camino and on life itself. The young German backpacker—tall, good-natured, and travelling lighter than seemed reasonable—refilled his bottle and prepared to continue to Roncesvalles, another twenty-six kilometres ahead. He was determined to push on, youth and enthusiasm driving him beyond Orisson and into the late afternoon sun. We said a brief goodbye. Nothing dramatic, just a handshake, a smile, a shared gratitude for the water that had saved us both. I watched him disappear along the path, his slight figure swallowed by the folds of the mountains. I assumed I would never see him again. And yet, in a curious twist of Camino fate, our paths crossed once more in Santiago—over a month later—after both our journeys had reached their end. We greeted each other like old friends, laughing at the coincidence and sharing stories of the roads we had walked in the days and weeks between.

Like ships passing in the night, our journeys had brushed against each other just long enough to leave an imprint. Such is the nature of the Camino. It gathers strangers for a moment, lets them touch one another's lives, and then sends them drifting on again—each carrying a small piece of the other.

Chapter 3. The Learning Curve.

Diary entry: The path from **Orisson to Roncesvalles** stretched out in long waves of green, speckled with wild horses and broken only by the wind drifting across the ridges. By the time the trail began its downward turn, my legs were aching, and the afternoon sun still pressed heavily on my back. Somewhere along the descent, instinct—or perhaps impatience—guided my steps. Instead of following the long arc of the official route, I spotted a narrow break in the grass, a steep gully that cut sharply down the mountainside. It looked like a shortcut, although there was no marker to confirm it. Without overthinking it, I followed. Down I went —carefully at first, then with growing confidence—sliding, stepping, and shifting my weight against the slope. When I rejoined the wider track below, it was obvious I had saved at least an hour of walking.

By early evening, I reached the great **Monastery of Roncesvalles,** its ancient stones cool, calm and solemn, offering rest to pilgrims as it had for centuries. I found my bed, washed my face, and let the fatigue of the day soften into quiet reflection.

It is only now, looking back from the distance of years, that I begin to understand the deeper purpose of that first Camino. At the time, I believed I needed a quest—something tangible and heroic to justify my journey. I had fixed in my mind the idea of searching for a "sword of discernment," a symbolic object that would, somehow, deliver clarity and purpose to my troubled life. That idea would later become the title of my first novel. But on the Camino itself, I was still too tangled in the world of goals, achievements, and outcomes to grasp the real work being done within me. In hindsight, my need for a sword was really a longing to cut myself free from the past—its wounds, its chaos, its shadows. What I truly needed was surrender. Not the defeatist kind, but the surrender that softens the heart and allows the soul to breathe again. Back then, I could not see it. I was still damaged, still wrestling with the inner debris of years lived out of balance. I wanted answers. I wanted certainty. I wanted a reason—something worldly, measurable, almost heroic—that would validate the journey I had thrown myself into. The Camino does not unfold as we expect. It teaches quietly, lesson by lesson.

Lifes learning does not come in a single day, and often we only understand those lessons much later, when we look back with clearer eyes and a steadier heart. We are all travellers on this ancient Way—following, in spirit at least, the path attributed to St James. Whether he walked it or not hardly matters. What matters is the echo of his story: a life lived not in boasting of faith, but in the doing of it. And there, even then, was a truth waiting for me. But I was too raw, too wounded, too busy chasing symbols to recognise it. Still, the Way was patient. It had only just begun to teach me.

Diary – A Quiet Turning Within;

Somewhere along the climb and descent today, perhaps in the silence between footfalls or in the steady rhythm of my breath, I sensed a shift within myself. It was not sudden—more like a soft opening, a loosening of something that had been tightly wound for years. I realised that I had finally embraced an inner truth: to be honest with myself, to stay open-minded, to be willing to grow, to stop worrying about every imagined outcome, and to accept life as it came. These were not grand promises, but gentle ones—simple, human, and long overdue.

As I walked, I could feel the coil inside me beginning at last to unwind. For so long, I had lived wound tight, braced against life, pushing forward with force, strength, drive, leadership, dogma, determination. Those old ways had once propelled me like an arrow aimed at some distant target. But they had also exhausted me, splintered me, driven me away from myself.

Now the Camino was teaching me a slower pace, a different kind of strength—one carried moment to moment, one breath at a time. I found myself relaxing into this new way, trusting in God without needing to define Him, trusting in the journey rather than trying to control it.

I began to see myself as an artist working with wood. In the past, I had often carved against the grain, impatient and forceful, and the result had been splinters—inner wounds that took years to heal. But now, at last, I was learning to work *with* the grain, to follow the natural line of my own spirit.

It felt as though I had stepped into a quiet river within myself. Instead of fighting the current, I was letting it carry me— calmly, gently, sure of its own direction. I knew that once I learned the drift of this inner flow, all I would need was the slightest touch of the rudder to stay on course.

Tonight, as I rest in the quiet of **Roncesvalles**, I feel the faint beginning of a new kind of peace. There was in me a sense of my selfishness. So many pilgrims outside the monastery had lined up three deep to get a bed for the night. The abbots had added an extra 70 beds in a recent extension to the basement, bringing the total to 370. [I knew not all pilgrims in the line would get a bed, but I hoped I would be one of those who did. To fill in time, I went to the head of the line to purchase my pilgrim's passport, the document that identified me as a pilgrim and thus granted me a discount for bed and breakfast.

I got the passport, but was soon ushered in ahead of the pilgrims waiting outside. I asked God to forgive me for my indiscretion. I justified it by recognising that I was still recovering from deep depression and anxiety, and a peace soon came over me.] Not a loud, triumphant peace—just a soft one, like a candle lit against the darkness. And for now, that is enough.

Diary – Roncesvalles to Zubiri

I woke early in the great stone hush of the monastery, stirred by the soft rustling of other pilgrims preparing for the day. The air was cool—almost cold—and it slipped through the dormitory like a blessing. Outside, the sky was a pale wash of morning blue, the forest waiting in stillness for our footsteps. With a simple breakfast inside me and my pack tightened for the day, I stepped into the soft light and began the long walk to Zubiri.

The path wound gently at first, through tall pines that stood like silent guardians along the trail. Birds sang in the early hours—short, bright notes that seemed to encourage us on our way. The forest floor was damp, the scent of moss and earth rich and comforting. For a time, I felt cocooned, sheltered as though the Camino itself was easing me into this new rhythm of life.

But soon enough, the terrain changed. The trail dipped and rose with unexpected sharpness, and my legs began to feel the weight of each descent. The temperature, according to my phone's water map, read 42 degrees Celsius, and I was already feeling the weight of an overburdened backpack. Loose stones shifted underfoot, and I found myself treading carefully, remembering the fall I'd had in Paris only days earlier. I walked with both caution and determination—a strange marriage, but one that seemed fitting for a pilgrim still learning to trust himself and the journey.

Along the way, I met other pilgrims, each lost in their own story. A brief greeting here, a shared laugh there. No deep conversations—just the quiet companionship of strangers walking in the same direction. It was enough.

I left Los Arcos just as the first light of morning brushed the rooftops, the streets quiet and still. With the albergue behind me and the open road ahead, I felt a calm determination settle into my steps. Today, we're promised long stretches across the vast plains of La Rioja, where vineyards dominate the vast landscape, and the horizon seems to stretch endlessly.

Midway through the day, the sun grew fierce, beating down through the breaks in the forest canopy. Sweat stung my eyes, but the rhythmic crunch of boots on gravel kept me steady. Again and again, the trail descended sharply, punishing the knees, testing resolve. I found myself leaning on the inner lessons of the past few days—patience, acceptance, the willingness to go with the flow rather than fight the mountain.

At last, I caught sight of Zubiri—its cluster of houses gathered along the river like a quiet welcome. The final descent into the town was steep and demanding, and I felt every jolt in my joints. But the moment my boots touched the flat path beside the river, relief washed over me.

Crossing the medieval bridge—the Puente de la Rabia—I paused for a moment, letting the significance of the day settle in. The river flowed beneath me with a steady, ancient certainty, and I felt something within me mirror that movement—a gentle, inner current carrying me forward.

In **Zubiri,** I found a small albergue, clean and straightforward. After washing the dust from my body and clothes, I sat with my diary. I tried to capture what the day had offered: fatigue, determination, moments of quiet beauty, and a deeper settling into the person I was becoming.

My legs ached. My shoulders throbbed. But inside, something felt lighter. If the road to Roncesvalles had begun the unwinding of the inner spring, then today's walk to Zubiri seemed to smooth its coils, teaching me once again to surrender to the rhythm of each step.

Tonight, as the river hums softly outside, I am content. Tomorrow the road will call again. I showered and changed. Venturing outside, it was now 9 p.m., and nothing was open in the village. The only place to eat was a bar. I ate the last of the soup served in my bowl, with a couple of bread rolls. The flies crawled all over it, but I didn't care. I just needed to eat and a bed, hopefully for a good night's sleep to dream with, then the peace of my ancestors watching over me.

Before setting out towards **Pamplona**, I realised I needed to deal with an increasingly unbearable problem—my second toe. The nail had split and curved inward during the last days of walking, and with every step, it felt as though a tiny devil was stabbing upward from beneath it. Each footfall became a reminder of the fragility of the body and, perhaps, the stubbornness of the mind that carries it.

I tried to ignore it, attempted to adjust my laces, my socks, my stride—anything to blunt the pain—but it only worsened. I knew that if I didn't act, the next ten days ahead would be misery, perhaps even jeopardise my Camino entirely.

So in a moment of equal parts resolve and frustration, I took my nail scissors, slid them beneath the offending nail, and tore the whole thing free. A crude operation, certainly not something a sensible person would recommend, but the relief was immediate. I cleaned the area thoroughly, applied antibiotic ointment, and wrapped it carefully in a fresh bandage. A brutal solution—but it worked. No more stabbing pain, no more grimacing with every step. (I would later discover that it took nearly two years for that nail to grow back, a small souvenir from the Way.)

As I finished bandaging the toe, I couldn't help but smile at the absurdity and the honesty of the moment. Camino life strips you down to basics—food, water, sleep, and the condition of your feet. And yet, beneath the practical lies something more profound. Removing that nail felt like a tiny act of surrender: ripping away what no longer served me, accepting what *was*, and trusting that the body would heal in its own good time. I laced my boots, stood up, and took a tentative step. Pain-free. A small victory, but on the Camino, these small victories keep you moving forward. And so, with one less toenail and a little more humility, I prepared for the long road ahead.

I left Zubiri early, stepping out of the albergue while the town was still wrapped in morning quiet. Mist hovered low along the river like a veil, softening the edges of the world. My legs were stiff from yesterday's punishing descents, but once I found my pace, the familiar rhythm returned—step, breath, step, breath—as a whispered prayer carried forward along the Camino's ancient spine.

The trail followed the river for a time, its steady murmur offering both companionship and calm. The scent of damp earth and eucalyptus drifted through the air. I felt strangely light-hearted, as though I had finally begun to accept that the Way asks only for presence, not performance. Soon the path rose again, winding through small hamlets and stretches of quiet woodland. A few pilgrims passed me; I passed a few others—no need for long conversations. A nod, a "Buen Camino," and we each continued on our own inner path.

The path wound gently through meadows and small hamlets—**Ilarratz, Eskiroz, Zuriain**—each one offering a glimpse into the quiet, unhurried rhythm of rural life. Farmers were already in their fields, the smell of freshly turned earth mixing with the cool air. Dogs barked without urgency, simply acknowledging my passing.

The walk was serene, but also a particular introspective pull. With each kilometre, the mind loosened its grip on old worries. Thoughts drifted toward gratitude—for the strength in your legs, for the kindness of strangers, for the simple miracle of being alive and moving forward.

By late morning, the climb toward **Larrasoaña** brought a more profound fatigue, yet a deeper sense of presence. Pilgrims clustered in small cafés for coffee and tortilla, sharing stories

in broken languages but unified by the same longing to belong to something ancient and meaningful. Then the landscape began to change. The path broadened, fields gave way to industrial edges, and the hum of city life grew stronger. You passed through the outskirts, where the modern world pushed gently against the old Camino, reminding you that pilgrimage is as much about contrast as continuity.

The first Camino milestone outside Zuribi indicated 21 km to the city centre of Pamplona. The day's walk on even ground, through soft, grassy pastures, and finally a concrete pathway towards the city made the going easier, despite the constant reminder of my backpack's weight as the straps bit into my shoulders. The thought of a previous day pilgrim's reminder: "No matter what distracts you, stay focused on the goal ahead." A place to rest my head for the night came to mind, as I had not booked ahead, and the city would be teeming with visitors for the running of the bulls celebration during the three-day Feast of St. Fermin. The answer came with Willie, an Irish writer, who walked with me for the remaining few kilometres to the outskirts of the city. He suggested I stay at the hotel where he had booked, and he was sure I would find a room there.

As I approached **Pamplona,** the first great city of the Camino, something within me stirred—a mixture of excitement and reverence. The streets widened, the buildings rose in grandeur, and life pulsed with a vibrancy that felt both invigorating and overwhelming after days in the quiet countryside.

Entering through the ancient gates, I became a part of the city's centuries-old story. Pamplona welcomed not with fanfare, but with a kind of noble familiarity, as if it had seen countless pilgrims cross its threshold and knew well the sacred fatigue written in their faces.

I wandered its narrow streets with Willie, tasted its food, and breathed in its history. As luck would have it, I acquired the room with some of Willie's Irish charm rubbing off on the proprietor. I lay on the bed for a short sleep and woke up an hour later. Willie had already gone out to meet friends, and as the evening settled, the city lights flickered on like a constellation brought down to earth. I made my way to a city bar and met up with two Irish ladies who rank copious quantities of white wine, calling out to the barman for another: " One more, no more." which they didn't live up to. I left them alcohol free and made my way back to the hotel.

In the back of my mind, the Camino was beginning to reveal something more profound: The journey is not only about reaching Santiago but about learning to arrive—fully, humbly—in each moment. [Such insights were always entered in my diary for future reference.]

Chapter 4. Symbols and Signs.

I had decided it was time to jettison the weight of my tent and a couple of kilos of unnecessary gear. Every step reminded me of those extra burdens strapped to my back. But because it was a holiday feast day, the *correo*—the post office—was closed. That meant another eighty kilometres of carrying what I no longer needed before I could finally send it away. In hindsight, I could have simply donated the whole lot to a local charity or left it for another pilgrim who needed it more.

Yet, even in this minor frustration, the Camino was teaching me. The journey, I was discovering, was not just about reaching Santiago—it was about learning to arrive long before the cathedral towers appeared. Each day carried its own quiet lessons. And this day's teaching was simple but profound: "less is more."A truth for my pack, and perhaps even more so for my life.

I left Pamplona early, the city still wrapped in the pale blue hush that comes before dawn. The streets were empty but for a street cleaner and a baker setting trays of fresh bread into his window. The smell was heavenly, and I bought a small loaf for the day's journey—*learning already to prepare, but not to overburden myself.*

At the bake house, I ordered a coffee and watched the morning news of a major train crash on the entry to Santiago railway station. It was packed with pilgrims, and many lives had been lost. I was feeling homesick for Australia, and called a friend back home to have a long conversation. He, too, had watched the news report on TV. Here today and gone tomorrow, entered my head as I trudged onward.

Pamplona to Puente la Reina – The Hill of Forgiveness

The path wound gently upward through the outskirts of the city before beginning its long climb towards the Alto del Perdón—the Hill of Forgiveness. I had heard of it many times before walking the Camino, always spoken of with a kind of reverence, as though it were not merely a physical ascent but a spiritual rite of passage. And perhaps it was.

When I reached the top, a small group of pilgrims stood gathered beside the iconic metal sculptures of ancient peregrinos leaning into the wind. The view swept out in all directions: villages tucked into folds of hills, dusty trails cutting across the land like lifelines. I stood in silence, letting the breeze wash over me. *Forgiveness. A word easier to write than to live.*

The morning sun broke over the ridges, casting long shadows across fields of wheat and wind turbines turning lazily in the distance. Each step seemed to echo something inside me. I felt the weight of the past, as though every unresolved hurt. The Camino was not about grasping, but about releasing, not about finding power, but surrendering it. A part of me wanted to leave something behind at **Alto del Perdón**—an offering, a token of the burdens I had carried too long. Instead, I simply closed my eyes and breathed out slowly, imagining old griefs dissolving into the wind. Whether they did or not is another question—but the intention was enough.

The descent on the far side was steep and treacherous, loose stones sliding underfoot. I found myself concentrating intensely, the physical demand pulling me back into reality.
From there, the walk rolled through small villages—**Uterga, Muruzábal**—and fields that shimmered with life. The world felt open, expansive, trusting. By afternoon, the elegant

silhouette of **Puente la Reina** appeared, its ancient Romanesque bridge stretching across the river like an invitation. Crossing that bridge, with its smooth, worn stones and centuries of pilgrim footsteps carved into its memory, felt like stepping into the long river of all who had walked before me.

I was smiling to myself now as I re-read those diary entries. Cats were one thing; the two-legged females I encountered in the years that followed that first Camino were another entirely. I could have done without many of those encounters. Instead, I surrendered—too readily at times—to their passions and persistent influences, much to my later regret.

Yet even in that admission, I can see the pattern the Camino was quietly teaching me: how easily I confuse surrender with compliance, and how lessons often arrive disguised as attraction rather than warning. The Camino had tried to teach me about surrender, but it would take years—and a fair amount of pain—before I understood the difference between surrender and self-betrayal.
I paused midway, leaning on the wall, watching the water slide beneath. Life does not rush, I realised. It flows.
And all we are asked to do is flow with it.

Present moment. A young woman from France slipped past me, and I turned with a smile. "Slowly," she warned, "the mountain likes to steal knees." Every fractured relationship, every disappointment—had climbed the hill with me. That evening in the albergue, after washing clothes and sharing a simple meal with other pilgrims, I recorded another line in my diary: *Today I forgave myself for not knowing better in the past. And in doing so, I felt the Way open a little wider before me.*

Estella to Los Arcos – Solitude and the Rhythm of the Way

The morning in Estella was soft, wrapped in the golden glow of dawn. The streets were quiet, the plaza still damp with dew, and the distant bells of the church rang their gentle call. I left the albergue with a light pack, a loaf of bread tucked inside, and a renewed sense of patience. Today promised a longer walk, more time with the road and my own thoughts, and I welcomed it.

The trail led out of town past the vineyards I had admired yesterday, and then into the open fields of **Navarra.** The landscape stretched wide and serene, with rolling hills and scattered farmhouses, dry stone walls tracing patterns across the sunlit earth. The solitude of the trail enveloped me, each footstep a meditation, each breath a quiet prayer.

The sun rose higher, warm and insistent, and I became aware of the small miracles of the Camino: a hidden fountain with clear, cool water; a gnarled tree offering welcome shade; the distant call of a shepherd's dog across the valley. These moments reminded me that even in simplicity, life provides sustenance, beauty, and small gestures of care.

Mid-morning brought a brief struggle. My water bottle ran dry, and for a moment the sun seemed to press down harder, the trail stretching endlessly ahead. But soon enough, a small farm appeared with a tap partially hidden by a row of shrubs. I drank deeply, grateful, and shared a smile with another pilgrim who had also paused. Even in the vastness, the Camino offers connection when we least expect it.

The approach to Los Arcos was gentle, the town's red-tiled roofs rising over the green fields like a quiet promise. The streets were narrow, winding, and full of character, each stone building whispering centuries of stories. I found the albergue, a small haven with the comforting murmur of other pilgrims in the background, all settling in for the evening after their own long day.

After a simple meal, I sat outside under the fading sun, writing in my diary: *"Today was long and hot, but full of quiet lessons. The Camino is teaching me to be patient, to accept what comes, to notice what I might otherwise overlook. Each step carries both the weight of the world and the lightness of being, if I allow it. Solitude is not loneliness—it is a conversation with the self, with the Way, with the life flowing beneath my feet."*

As night fell, the streets emptied, the stars began to pierce the dark, and I felt the Camino's rhythm settle deep within me. The next day promised another stretch, another chance to learn the slow, patient art of walking, surrendering, and arriving.

Another diary note: "The Camino teaches perseverance in its simplicity: keep walking, keep noticing, keep surrendering. Each step is both a lesson and a gift. Today, across the plains and vineyards, I felt the patience of the earth, the persistence of the vine, and a growing steadiness within myself. The Way flows through everything, and I am learning to move with it."

Night fell softly, stars prickling the sky above the city, and I felt both the fatigue and quiet satisfaction of a day well walked. Tomorrow promised more vineyards, more fields, and more lessons in letting go and trusting the Way.

Los Arcos to Logroño – Plains, Vineyards, and Perseverance.

The trail flowed gently, punctuated by occasional farmhouses and the distant hum of tractors. Rows of vines stretched in perfect lines, their leaves shimmering in the rising sun. I marvelled at the careful, patient labour that had gone into these fields, and somehow it mirrored the patience I was learning to cultivate within myself. Each step on the Camino, each hour of walking, felt like its own careful tending of spirit.

Midway through the day, the sun pressed down relentlessly. My pack felt heavier than ever, but I reminded myself of the lesson I had learned in Pamplona: *less is more.* Each step became a meditation in itself, a rhythm of breath and movement, noticing the wind on my face, the crunch of gravel beneath my boots, the distant call of a bird tracing the vast sky.

By late afternoon, the towers and red roofs of Logroño emerged, the city bustling with life after the long solitude of the plains. Entering through its streets felt like stepping into another world: cafes spilling into plazas, bicycles clattering over cobbles, voices.

In the albergue, after washing and resting, I wandered through the old quarter. The churches, the stone streets, the fountains —all seemed imbued with the weight of centuries of pilgrims who had walked before me. And yet, tonight, it felt uniquely mine.

Logroño to Nájera – Along the Ebro, Rivers and Reflection

I left Logroño in the soft light of dawn, the city still stirring, its streets empty save for early bakers and a few fellow pilgrims on the same path. The air was fresh, carrying hints of vineyards and fertile earth. I felt the rhythm of the Camino settle into me once again—step, breath, step, breath—a cadence as old as the Ebro River for much of the day, its waters glinting in the sun, reflecting both the sky above and the journey within. Walking beside it, I felt a quiet companionship with the river—always moving, constantly flowing, never stopping to dwell on the past or anticipate the future. A gentle reminder that the Camino, like the river, carries you forward whether you are ready or not.

The vineyards stretched endlessly along the plains, rows of green and gold folding into one another under the warm sun.
 I paused often to drink water, feel the sun on my skin, and notice the small gifts of the trail: the sound of birds, the hum of distant farm life, and the brief companionship of a fellow pilgrim at a hidden fountain. These moments, fleeting yet profound, reminded me that the Camino is as much about noticing and surrendering as it is about moving forward.

Arriving in **Nájera** in the late afternoon, I was greeted by the town's quiet charm and the dignified presence of the monastery of Santa María la Real. Sitting in the albergue that evening, I reflected in my diary: *"Each step carries meaning when taken with attention and surrender. The Camino is not about speed or distance, but about presence, patience, and the quiet gifts along the way."* Night fell gently, and the stars above promised another day of discovery and inward journey toward Santo Domingo de la Calzada. So it was that I wrote more notes into my diary, signs and symbols of the past now gone, but now happy to recall

Just as pilgrims pause to note each stone marker, I too can acknowledge the small victories in my own journey of The Way—moments when I chose compassion over frustration, patience over fear."

Each step I take carries meaning. The milestones on the path remind me that progress, however small, is still progress. Every stone marker tells a story of endurance, of a pilgrim who paused, looked around, and kept moving forward. In my own life, these moments are mirrored in every act of patience, every choice to respond with care rather than fear.

The scallop shells worn into the ground speak softly of guidance. Their grooves draw water to the centre, just as the journey draws me inward, toward my own heart. They remind me that even when the road is heavy or uncertain, there is direction, a rhythm to follow, a way forward.

Milestones: *"Every small step counts. Pause, notice your progress, and honour each moment of endurance."*

One small step is enough.

Scallop Shells: *"Even worn and weathered, guidance is present. Follow the path your heart shows, one step at a time."*

I am guided even when the path seems unclear.

Carvings on Rocks: *"Your actions leave marks, seen and unseen. Kindness, love, and boundaries endure beyond the moment."*

What I feel today will leave a gentle mark.

Village Churches & Crosses: *"There are many ways to hope and express care. Find your own way, and honour the journey.*

There are many ways to hold hope, and I will honour mine.

Way Markers & Arrows: *"Signs appear when you need direction. Trust the guidance within and around you."*

Direction will reveal itself- move forward calmly.

Rivers, Stones, Bridges: *"Obstacles can be crossed, paths can be navigated. Patience and care carry you forward."*

I can cross what challenges me. I stay grounded, steady, and present.

Pilgrim Staff: *"Support and self-care are essential. Rest, ask for help, and protect your wellbeing."*

It's strong to lean on help.

Nature Along the Way: *"Growth, endurance, and beauty exist even amid hardship. Stand rooted, reach toward light."*

Reflection: *"I am here. I am moving forward. I am not lost. I am doing the best I can, and that is enough."*

Light finds me even through the trees.

These positive notes in my diary were enough to sustain me, like water for a thirsty man. Closing my diary in the present day, closed my eyes, and soon I slept, dreaming of a journey along the cobblestone path of The Way.

On reflection, I attempted to reason my way out of the memories of recent tragedies that finally led me to the Camino. I wanted release—some way to let go—and jotting down my daily entries helped, at least emotionally. I did not come to follow the Way of St. James. Yes, tradition tells that his remains were set adrift Viking-style across the waters and came to rest on the Iberian Peninsula, later discovered some eight hundred years after his death and used symbolically by Christian leaders to rally support and funds during the wars with the Moors. But I never quite accepted that version of events. St. James was not my concern. My pilgrimage was not about venerating a martyr but about unburdening my own life.

If I were to surrender, it would be to a God of my own understanding—not to St. James, nor to the doctrines built around him.

Yet the fact remained: I was walking a road that millions had walked before me for more than a thousand years, seeking meaning, healing, penitence, hope. What drew me most were the myths, the legends, the folklore woven through the land. And slowly, almost without my noticing, something within me began to shift—strange stirrings, quiet recognitions, small awakenings.

I found myself craving spiritual solace. It became my daily ritual to step inside the church of every village where I stayed. Those dim, cool spaces gave me a chance to unwind, to reflect on the day's journey, to breathe and pray before I looked for a bed for the night or a simple meal. In those moments of stillness, I began to sense that the Camino—as ancient, symbolic, and mysterious as it was—had started its work within me.

Chapter 5. A New Realisation.

Perhaps it began with the simple rhythm of walking—the metronome of the feet, the breath, the heartbeat. Maybe it was the silence between villages. Or the faces of strangers who somehow felt familiar. Or the mornings when the sun rose through the mist and the world looked new again. Whatever it was, I found myself drawn—almost magnetically—to the spiritual spaces along the Way. It became my habit, practically a necessity, to enter the church in every village where I stayed, not out of obligation, but out of longing. Those cool stone interiors held a kind of stillness I didn't know I was missing. I'd sit in the silence, letting the day fall away. My thoughts would settle. My breathing would slow. And in that quiet, I would find a small moment of peace. I would reflect on the day's walk, the conversations with other pilgrims, the aches in my body, and the stirrings in my heart. I would whisper a prayer—not always with words, sometimes only with feeling —and then step back into the world to find a meal and a bed for the night.

I wasn't a traditional pilgrim. I wasn't seeking indulgences or absolution or the favour of a saint. But the Way seemed to have its own ideas. It worked on me quietly, gradually, through symbols older than Christianity and stories older still. It invited me to surrender—not to a doctrine, but to the journey itself. To the healing found in movement, in solitude, in companionship, in the land, and in the ancient human need to walk toward something unknown.

I came to the Camino to escape my memories. Instead, I found a place where I could finally face them, gently, step by step. It was not St. James who led me here. It was something more profound, older, more personal—something that whispered through the myths and the stones:

Walk. Feel. Let the past loosen its hold. And trust that the road will do the rest.

It was like seeing through a glass darkly—muted, distorted, incomplete—yet still enough to sense that something was waiting for me ahead. A promise. A possibility. A future I had not dared to imagine. And in the mystery of my own mind, somewhere between the steps, the poems, and the silent conversations with the horizon, I began to see it: a glimmer of light at the end of the tunnel. Not a blaze. Not a miracle. Just a light—small, steady, and mine.

It was as though I were walking a tightrope along this spiritual way of pilgrimage—mindful of every step I took. I lived somewhere between darkness on one side and light on the other, between the pure heart I longed to reclaim and the shadow self shaped by worldliness that had once guided my former life, before the fall into a pit of despair that nearly consumed me.

As I reread my diary from that journey of letting go—layer upon layer of buried dead, pain, and suffering from the previous decade—I could see more clearly what had been happening within me. The Camino was not only beneath my feet; it was unfolding inside my mind and heart. Each step became a quiet negotiation between who I had been and who I was becoming. Yet there was also the undeniable reality of the Camino itself. It was no abstract spiritual idea. It was rugged mountain tracks that burned the legs and tested resolve. It was long valley floors that stretched patience and endurance. It was open fields of grass where the wind carried silence, and cobblestone streets laid down by Roman hands centuries before my own. It was highways and backroads, the hum of modern traffic giving way to the hush of ancient byways. It was the occasional stream to cross, stones slippery beneath tired boots, demanding balance and attention.

In a single day, I might pass through a modern city alive with noise and urgency, then enter an ancient village seemingly untouched by time. Of such was my own state too, mirroring my inner journey—moving constantly between the present world and something far older, more profound, and more enduring.

The Camino held all of it at once: hardship and beauty, noise and stillness, despair and hope. And as I walked that tightrope —between shadow and light—I began to understand that the path was not asking me to choose one side over the other. It was asking me to remain present, to keep my balance, and to trust that each careful step forward was, in itself, an act of healing.

It was the writing that kept me steady—the jotting down of memories from the trail, the brief encounters with fellow pilgrims, the faces and conversations that flickered in and out of my days like passing lanterns. I wrote poems too, ones that arrived unannounced, as if carried by the same wind that swept across the wheat fields. They came out of the blue, surprising even me, as though some dormant part of my mind had finally found its voice.

The physical challenge became its own meditation. Each day brought the same rhythm: the early morning chill, the tightening straps of the backpack, the first deliberate steps forward. At first, it was sheer endurance—blisters, sore knees, the ache in my shoulders. But soon, the walking entered a different register. It became meditative. A steady heartbeat. A slow unwinding. The mind, given enough distance and daylight, began to loosen its knots.

In that repetition, in that quiet grind of one foot after the other, I began to sense something shifting inside me. At first, it was faint—almost imperceptible. A moment of clarity here, a strange calm there. But slowly, unmistakably, I recognised that I was emerging from a dark place. Not with a fanfare, not with some grand revelation, but with a subtle awareness that the grip of fear had loosened.

I was no longer standing in the dragon's mouth—the place where death wishes, and despair had once circled me like smoke. Instead, a new way of seeing was forming within me, fragile but real. An awakening. A slight, bright edge of hope.

I came across a note in my diary, written without polish but heavy with truth: *Everything happens for a reason. Nothing occurs by chance, nor by good or bad luck alone. Illness, injury, love, loss, moments of greatness, and even sheer stupidity—all arise to test the limits of our soul. Without these tests, life would be a smooth, paved, flat road leading nowhere. Safe and comfortable, perhaps—but dull, pointless, and ultimately meaningless.*

When someone hurts us, betrays us, or breaks our heart, we are invited to learn forgiveness—not as weakness, but as liberation. When someone loves us, we are called to love in return. In all our dealings with others, we learn to be as vigilant as a flame-wise serpent, and as gentle as a dove.
Love, when it matures, becomes unconditional—but boundaries must remain conditional, to protect ourselves and those we care for.
Rereading those words, I realised I had not written them as philosophy. They were born of experience—earned through

pain, walking, reflection, and the slow work of letting go. Somewhere between the miles and the memories, the Camino had been teaching me not how to avoid suffering, but how to be shaped by it without being destroyed.

Only later did I understand what was happening. At the time, I was simply walking—placing one foot in front of the other, recording the day's miles, easing the ache in my body, emptying my mind onto the page each evening. I had come to let go, nothing more. To loosen the grip of grief and survive the weight of what had been.

Yet the Camino was offering more than release. It was quietly schooling me in a way of being. The suffering I carried, the symbols I encountered, and the rhythm of the road itself were not separate experiences but part of a single unfolding lesson. Walking became prayer. Fatigue became honesty. The landscape—its stones, shells, churches, and crossings — became a language through which something older and wiser spoke.

I did not arrive at sudden certainty or dramatic revelation. What emerged was gentler: an awakening that moved at a walking pace. A growing awareness that life could be lived more consciously, more creatively, more truthfully. That meaning was not found at the end of the road, but shaped slowly in the act of walking it.

Unbeknownst to me at the time, the Camino was introducing me to the life that would follow. The letting go was only the beginning. The discipline of reflection, the acceptance of struggle, the reverence for symbol and story—all of it would later shape my creativity and give rise to a new way of living: a quieter path, perhaps, but one rich with purpose.

The realisation dawned on me then that the people I had met and the successes and failures I had experienced through them helped shape who I was becoming. Every challenging experience carried a lesson; in fact, I realised that, through my life, the hardest lessons had proved most important on my soul's journey.

Here, on the Camino, I made a simple but profound resolution: to make every day count, to appreciate every moment, and to take from the experience everything I possibly could—for my own benefit and for that of the pilgrims whose paths crossed mine. I knew, with a certainty that surprised me, that I might never walk this way again. The people I met each day on the road, I might never see again, either.

Taking the time to listen to them became an education in itself. When I stopped long enough to hear their stories truly, I realised how much wisdom travels quietly alongside us, waiting only for our attention. In listening, I was learning—not just about others, but about myself.

It was then that another truth began to surface: I could make of life what I chose. I was not bound to the patterns of my former life, nor limited by what I had once believed possible. I would create my own future. I would make a difference. It was a far-reaching vision—one I would never have imagined before the fall, before the long descent into despair that had preceded this walk.

I resolved to live without regret. If I loved someone, I would let that person know. If someone troubled me, I would speak honestly, giving them—and myself—the dignity of truth and the opportunity for change. The Camino was teaching me that clarity, when offered with respect, is an act of kindness.

Strangely, as I walked on, thoughts returned to those I had loved and those who had shaped my life in earlier years. People from the past rose gently into memory—not with bitterness, but with understanding. I could see more clearly how each encounter, each wound, each kindness had played its part in shaping the person I was becoming.

The road had not erased my history. It had given it meaning.
And so I walked on—lighter, more awake, carrying forward not answers, but intentions. The Camino had shown me that life, like the path itself, is created step by step. And from that moment on, I chose to walk it consciously.
I journaled every day of my life on the Camino. At the time, I believed it was an effort of the rational mind—an attempt to reason my way toward what I assumed were spiritual answers. Looking back, I see it differently. The writing was not about solving anything; it was about making space. Each page became a quiet act of release.

Through those daily entries, I began to loosen my grip on pain and suffering. I wrote simple, positive mantras—words of intention, words of detachment—from the troubles of the past. The journal became both anchor and compass: a place to let go, and a place to record where I was, both inwardly and in the real, physical world unfolding around me.
It was as much about release as it was about remembrance. I captured the details of the journey—the changing landscapes, the weight of the pack, the rhythm of walking—and, just as importantly, the people. The pilgrims I met along the Way, each carrying their own stories, became part of my own unfolding narrative. Their presence, their conversations, their kindnesses were written into those pages alongside my own reflections.

In writing it all down, I was not chasing enlightenment. I was learning attentiveness. I was learning how to be present—to the road beneath my feet, to the strangers beside me, and to the slow, quiet transformation taking place within. The journal did not give me answers. It gave me clarity. And in that clarity, something essential was already changing.

The following pages of my diary carried me inward, into long stretches of reflection. I found myself contemplating those who had passed from this earth—people who had left a profound imprint on my life. In those moments, the immediate reality of the journey before me sometimes faded. The road continued beneath my feet, but my mind wandered through memory, loss, and gratitude.

At one point, I drifted off the Camino itself. Lost in thought, I followed a path that felt right until it quietly wasn't. It was only when I reached a crossroads that I emerged from that dreamlike state and realised I was no longer where I should be. There was no sign, no arrow, no reassurance—only uncertainty.

Standing at that crossroads, uncertain and alone, I recognised the pattern. I had been here before in life—moving without direction, trusting habit instead of awareness, allowing thought to replace presence. The Camino had simply made it visible.

Finding my way back by trial and error felt earned. Each wrong turn corrected, each step retraced, required humility and patience. There was no guide to consult, no voice to reassure me—only the quiet instruction to slow down, to look more, and so, by trial and error, I found my way back. I retraced my steps, listened more carefully, paid closer attention. I had no map and no guiding hand to consult, only my instincts and a growing awareness that presence mattered. It was a slight disorientation, yet it carried its own lesson.

When I reached the next large town, I resolved to buy an English-translated guidebook. Not because I had lost trust in myself, but because I understood the value of support. Even pilgrims need guidance. At the very least, I had my phone if things went awry, but I no longer wished to rely solely on chance.

That moment on the road mirrored something deeper. Reflection is necessary, but so is attentiveness. Memory has its place, but the path demands presence. The Camino was teaching me—quietly, patiently—that to walk well, one must balance inner wandering with outer awareness. And when lost, the simple act of stopping, noticing, and asking for direction is often enough to bring us home again.

My day began in semi-darkness. I set out early, heading for the next village a few kilometres down the track, drawn by the simple morning ritual of freshly squeezed orange juice, strong coffee, and warm croissants. It was a small comfort, but one that carried me forward. From there, I tramped along wide farm tracks through open fields of green and rows of grapevines, covering the long twenty-one kilometres from Nájera to Santo Domingo. The day grew hot quickly, and shade was scarce. The sun pressed down relentlessly, turning each step into an endurance test.

Water became precious. At **Azofra,** 5.8 kilometres in, and again at **Cirueña**, 9.5 kilometres along the way, I found relief. The town square fountains felt like oases in the desert, allowing me to refill my bottles and cool my hands and face. These fountains and monuments appeared faithfully in towns and villages along the direct route of the Camino—quiet, practical symbols of care left by those who had walked before.

Each stop was brief, but essential. It marked not just distance covered, but survival, generosity, and the unspoken understanding that the road is shared. I moved on lighter, steadier, grateful for water, for shade when it appeared, and for the simple mercy of a path that, though demanding, always seemed to offer what was needed at just the right moment.

Another strange happening I noticed on the Camino was when I handed over to a power within without definition, and just let everything unfold of its own accord. Wonderful things occurred. One of these happenings was when I went to look for a travel guidebook on the Camino in **San Domingo.** I had just begun walking the streets in the hope of finding an information centre to help me when I happened upon a Spanish bookshop.

At the front window display sat the only English-language guidebook in the store, and it was just what I had visualised. It proved to be a treasure trove of information, including topographic maps of the route to Santiago, accommodation sites, and tourist attractions along the way.

Chapter 6. Mindfulness.

I had read in the diary of my entry to **San Dominico.** Buying the guidebook as I headed to a nearby bookshop on the way to the city's Central Square was not an admission of failure. It was an act of maturity. I understood then that surrender did not mean walking unthinkingly. It meant knowing when to trust intuition and when to accept guidance. Independence and support were not opposites; they were companions on the road.

From that point on, I walked differently. I still reflected, still carried memory and loss with me, but I stayed present to the path beneath my feet. I paid attention to the signs, the arrows, the subtle cues of the land. I learned that wandering inward without grounding leads to confusion, but reflection held in balance with awareness leads to insight.

That crossroads marked a quiet shift. I had not just found the Camino again—I had reclaimed my place on it. And in doing so, I understood something essential: the Way does not require perfection, only presence. When we lose our way, it is not punishment but invitation—an invitation to wake up, to choose again, and to walk on with intention.

I finished that chapter of my journey believing I had merely survived a dark passage of my life. Only with time did I realise I had been given something far greater: a way forward. A way of walking. And the first fragile steps toward a legacy I had not yet imagined. My mind drifted now to a note I had written to a friend who was suffering much due to life circumstances.

" The tightrope we walk of past and present viewing positive or negative outlook, or leaning to the light or dark within, is ours as a matter of choice. It is always ours to decide which way to view, dig into or leave alone. I see it as a balancing act to walk the thin, narrow spiritual path of desired circumstance. The spiritual path encourages us to dig deep if we are to be released from evil, be it past, present, or, if we choose to speculate, future. We suffer to change, give to receive, and hand over to overcome. Much have we suffered by the actions of others, and indeed, your own, over a lifetime. We need not allow the evil intent or the influences of others in the past to coerce us into personality copying or duplicative actions. We are highly conscious beings in our dotage if we allow ourselves to be, and we have the gift of God's grace to lead us in accord with his will, as a guiding plan for living a good life here. "

I could relate my spiritual inward path to the Way I now walk upon this earthly realm, in accord with my spiritual learning, as I let go of all the sorrow and pain of recent years on that way to Santiago.

I was just over a week into the Camino now, and I noted in my diary that I had started early. Before leaving **Santo Domingo de la Calzada,** I set out to find an ATM. With minimal cash left, I settled instead at a small sidewalk café for breakfast and asked the young waitress for help. She kindly led me to a nearby ATM and assisted me in withdrawing money with my travel card. I paid for my breakfast, grateful for her quiet generosity, and soon set off on the next leg of the journey toward **Belorado**.

At a small roadside stall in **Grañón**, I bought some fruit to carry me through the remainder of the day's walk. I refilled my water bottles from a nearby fountain and spoke briefly with the stall-holder, who warned me that although it was still early, the temperature had already reached thirty-six degrees Celsius. The sky was a clear, unbroken blue—no promise of cloud or rain. It was not encouraging news, particularly knowing that much of the day's route would run alongside a busy highway.

As the hours passed, the heat intensified, and the continual pounding of my feet against the hard path and road surface began to take its toll. Blisters flared, and each step grew more deliberate. Yet I kept walking, aware that the Camino was once again stripping things back to essentials—water, shade, endurance, and patience. There was no room for hurry, only the steady act of putting one foot in front of the other and trusting that the road, however unforgiving, would carry me forward.

My mind drifted to Shirley MacLaine's book and her Camino journey as I entered **Viloria de Rioja**. I recalled her fear of dogs, and the stories she told of vicious packs encountered along the Way. The tales spoke of dogs attacking like wolves —or dingoes back home—moving together with an unnerving instinct. Foncebadón, a remote mountain village, was often spoken of as the place where that fear felt most real. It had gained a reputation for packs of dogs roaming the area, and for pilgrims who had been attacked or chased along the approach. But Foncebadón was still a couple of weeks away, and so, for now, those thoughts passed through my mind without troubling me. At this point in my journey, they were merely stories carried on the wind of the Camino.

The dogs I encountered on the Camino barked a little, but for the most part, they simply lay about, looking sad and half-dead in the heat of the Spanish drought. They seemed more weary than threatening, conserving what little energy they had left. Cats, however, are another matter for me. I am not a cat person—yet there has never been a time when cats were not drawn to me. Put me in a room full of people with one or two cats, and somehow they will always find their way to where I am sitting. My travels on the Camino were no exception. These days, I have learned to accept it. I stroke their fur, listen to them purr, and surrender to the inevitable attention. Still, if I am honest, I would much prefer to keep my distance. Dogs are more my go and far more faithful. At least in my experience, it had been so.

As I entered the village of **Viloria de Rioja,** I made my way to the fountain in the square and filled my water flasks for the next leg of the journey. I then sat on a nearby bench beneath the shade of a tree, enjoying some bread and the last of the fruit and nuts from my backpack. From my recently acquired guidebook, I knew there were still more than eight kilometres to walk to Belorado in the extreme heat, before crossing into the region of Castilla y León. For a moment, I settled into the quiet pleasure of the bench, the shade, and the simple meal spread before me. Then, without warning, my solitude was broken. A large number of feral cats suddenly invaded my area.

They seemed to appear from every doorway, nook, and cranny of the village square. I glanced along the street and saw even more emerging from shadowed entrances, all of them making their way toward me with quiet determination. I couldn't help but wonder whether my earlier thoughts of Shirley MacLaine and her fear of dogs, and the many strange stories told along the Camino, were now circling back to meet me. Or perhaps my own long-held disdain for these feline creatures was being gently challenged—a small lesson from the universe, delivered not with menace, but with whiskers and watchful eyes. Cats-They seemed to appear from every doorway, nook, and cranny of the village square. I looked down the street and saw even more slipping out from shadowed entrances, all of them converging on me as if summoned.

I began to wonder whether my earlier thoughts of Shirley MacLaine and her fear of dogs, and the many strange stories carried along the Camino, were now being answered in their own peculiar way. Perhaps the universe, having noted my general indifference—if not outright resistance—to cats, had decided to offer me a gentle lesson in acceptance. Not wolves. Not wild dogs. Just a quiet feline committee, assembled to test my capacity for surrender. It seemed the Camino, once again, had a sense of humour.

As a rather large cat leapt onto the bench beside me, I quickly packed up my food and belongings and exited stage right. The cat meowed, screeched, and made a clumsy jump at the tree, barely catching itself, claws digging into the bark as it scrambled up to a branch. Meanwhile, an older man appeared, surrounded by yet more cats, carrying a skinny, sickly-looking kitten. He went to the bench I had just vacated, and instantly all the cats gathered around him. I guessed this was some kind of daily ritual in the village—just not the place to be for someone like me, who felt as though a fur ball had lodged firmly in the throat.

I trudged along the road until I found another quiet spot where I could finally finish my lunch in peace. I couldn't help but laugh. Perhaps the Camino was reminding me, in its own peculiar way, that surrender comes in many forms—not just to grand vistas or fellow pilgrims, but even to the unexpected wisdom of cats and the quiet patience of an older man with a kitten. However, more cats emerged from doorways as the homeowners let them out for a while. Resigned to the fact that

I had no choice if I wished to escape, I left the village without finishing my lunch.

My mind drifted back to Shirley MacLaine and her encounters with vicious dogs. She had walked her Camino in the summer of her sixty-ninth year—my age at the time of writing my diary—a decade before I faced the feline onslaught. I would have much preferred to share in Shirley's tales of dogs, but Foncebadón, that dreaded village, was still ahead.

I vowed then and there not to dwell on cats or vicious dogs, focusing instead on my Camino, lest I unwittingly manifest some calamity I would later regret. As it turned out, Foncebadón held a different kind of trial—one that left a lingering discomfort and a miracle in a way, long after I had completed the Way. More on that will unfold in later dairy records.

As for the cats and vicious dogs, I distracted myself by reflecting on the lessons I had learned so far, and the strange, patient ways the Camino continued to teach surrender—even if it came in the form of whiskers, claws, or small-town rituals.

If I had been asked at that point what I wanted from the future, I could not honestly have answered. At least, not truthfully. Looking back through my diary now, the answers are there, written between the lines, but they were not what I believed I was searching for at the time. On the surface, I thought I wanted to be restored to health and happiness, and to find myself in the company of beautiful women.

In time, much of that did come to pass—but it took far longer than I imagined—more than one Camino. And even then, it was not what truly mattered. What lay ahead at Foncebadón was something else entirely. It was not what I was seeking, not what I expected, and not what I thought I needed. Yet it would change my life forever.

The moments turned into days, and each step became a kind of meditative freedom in the heat of the savage Spanish sun. As I walked, I repeated different mantras—at least, that is what my diary entries later reminded me. One of them returned again and again: *I am willing not to be me.*

The old me was living with the consequences of the life I had known until then. What was emerging was something more profound—the me of heart and soul, shaped by lessons I did not yet fully understand, but was clearly being prepared to become. It was not the words written in the diary that changed me; it was the experience of the Way itself. And even then, it was not so much what I encountered, but what I *felt* that mattered. Yes, I was willing not to be the old me, and in time —through patience and discipline—that willingness would begin to take form as reality. I had been conditioned into a false self. It had felt safe. The invention of a shadow self was easier to live with than facing who I was truly meant to become.

A new mantra was emerging at the time; I had written in my diary, and the words jumped from that page: "Hurry up and die, hurry up and die, so that you may live!"

Slowly, I was learning to walk despite that conditioning, to detach from the artificial self. When pain or sorrow surfaced, I learned to ride with the feeling, then gently detach from it, before returning to what I sensed I was becoming. Another me was my way of the Way. And it became a greater teacher and role model than anything I had ever encountered before.

The road to Santiago is always full of mystery and coincidence. Once again, I heard a quiet voice within me, a message I recognised as an old friend of the past, Christine's: *"You are building an unshakable faith. Be furnishing the quiet places of your soul now. Fill them with all that is harmonious and good, beautiful and enduring. Home is being built in the spirit, and the waiting will be well spent."*
For me, Christine was both guide and guardian angel in my greatest hour of need. She offered love and understanding at a time when I was slowly learning to let go of my ego and surrender to something more profound.

I was recalling the many encounters I had with pilgrims of 'The Way,' signs and symbols of friendship of the past. I had reached Ages, after 518 kms over mountains, hills and valleys, and across desert plains in the heat of that Spanish summer. There was still a long road ahead of me in life's journey, a long way to go as a pilgrim—and still a long road to Santiago.

I recall it all now as a cathartic, threshold moment before Foncebadón, when a new way of life for me would begin, and a new chapter in my life would unfold. I turned the page in my diary and looked ahead to the day's journey—from **Belorado** to the monastery of **San Juan de Ortega,** some twenty-five kilometres away. Here I was to discover more notes I had written:

"Pay attention to the thoughts and ideas that come to you. These thoughts are answers to your prayers for guidance. Be mindful of the doors that are opening and shutting, walk through the doors that open and learn from the doors that shut, your prayers are being answered… ."

"Don't try to force open the doors that appear closed to you. Instead, ask for guidance, and see if the doors are closed because of negative expectations, or it's simply a sign of timing."

"Take care of your physical body, eat healthy foods, exercise regularly and avoid toxins. Your body will emanate harmony, and if you follow the guidance, you will feel terrific… increased energy and happiness are your reward."

"Take steps right now to create time for relaxation. Don't allow yourself to be swayed on important issues."

"When you are ready, new blessings will come to you in life."

 "It's important to express your feelings; the more you release, the freer you will feel."

"Be careful of self-destructive tendencies, which come as misguided guilt. Help is there whenever you need it. Your desired outcome will come in the near future. Yes, you will receive your wish. Patience and positive thinking are what you need."

I had tramped the 25 km through the village of **Ages** towards the long dirt track to San Juan de Ortega. I referenced my dairy once again: "Legend credits San Juan de Ortega, a disciple of Santo Domingo, with clearing a path through the dense undergrowth of oak and pine."

I consulted about entry in my diary at the time: **San Juan de Ortega** (c. 1080–1163) was a Spanish hermit, monk, and engineer, best known for his devoted service to pilgrims on the Camino de Santiago. A disciple of **Santo Domingo de la Calzada**, Juan de Ortega dedicated his life to improving the safety of the Camino through the wild and dangerous **Montes de Oca**.

Looking at my travel guide, I noted that San Juan de Ortega founded a small monastery and hospice where pilgrims could find food, rest, and protection. His work transformed a perilous stretch of the Way into one marked by care and welcome. He is most famous today for the **Romanesque church at San Juan de Ortega** and the *"Miracle of the Light,"* when sunlight at the equinoxes illuminates sculpted biblical scenes—seen by many pilgrims as a sign of divine harmony and grace.

As for **angels**, tradition and Camino lore do suggest that Juan de Ortega was **divinely assisted** in his labours. While not documented as literal angelic intervention in a historical sense, stories speak symbolically of heavenly help guiding his work—reflecting the medieval belief that acts of compassion and service to pilgrims were undertaken in partnership with the divine.

Chapter 7-A Pilgrim's Blessing.

I often stopped to rest beneath the trees, grateful for the shade and silently thankful to San Juan for his efforts—and for the companionship of Raimon, the funny man who was forever stopping to smell the flowers. Raimon would pause to study leaves, peer into the undergrowth, or kneel beside some small wonder that had caught his eye. No matter how far behind I fell, even at my slow pace that day, I always managed to catch up. At our last rest stop before San Juan de Ortega, he lingered longer than usual, excited by the discovery of a four-leaf clover. I left him there on the track, delighted with his find. We met again a day later in Burgos, where he presented me with a symbolic gift of reasoned insight.

The trail crossed the remote **Oca Hills**, a route long infamous since medieval times for thieves and rogues who once hid among the trees. Yet my experience of the Way, especially along this stretch, could not have been more different. What had once been feared now felt peaceful and safe, as if the Camino itself was quietly reminding me that the dangers we inherit from the past do not always belong to the present. On a side road, I walked past a monument to the thirty-three men who had been taken to this location and shot, as traitors, by General Franco during the Spanish revolution. The walk to this spot was arduous, lengthy and dusty, although it was close to a forest on both sides of the track. I escaped the heat to a spot under a tree to contemplate the words on the monument, roughly translated as, "It is not for what they died, but how they died."

The track from the monument to the monastery was my next port of call; 8.6 km of pain eased somewhat by a small, flowing stream under a walkway, where I soaked my blistered, aching feet. This habit of washing my feet became a ritual along the way to Santiago. I didn't care if it was water from a ditch along a road or chemical water draining from a recently soaked paddock. At the time, it eased my pain, but the aftermath was a skin infection that lasted for some years, and no amount of doctoring could heal i; it just had to run its course and time to cure, much like the pain in my heart from so much tragic loss over the years, much of which was self-inflicted too.

The sight of the **San Juan de Ortega monastery** was a welcome one. The whole area consisted of a monastery which doubled as an albergue, attached to an L-shaped chapel where the body of San Domingo's disciple, San Juan, lay in an exposed tomb. Nearby stood the only other building, a café, also an extension of the monastery. I quickly showered, changed into fresh clothes, and put on sandals for my poor, wounded feet.

Once again, I was surprised to find the two Canadian school teachers in the dormitory. They were the angels who had given me Rosary beads to pray a mantra of 'Hail Marys.' I never got around to doing that, for I lost them the very next day. They invited me to join them at the Mass, which was about to start in the monastery. Although the Mass was in Spanish, I understood the sacred ceremony, having been educated in the Latin Mass as a child, and the Spanish didn't seem to differ much from the Latin I remembered from so many years before. After the Mass, we adjourned to a side altar where the body of the Saint is interred, and the priest read the Pilgrim's Blessing and the Pilgrim's Prayer to St. James. It was all very moving, and a timely reminder of the purpose of my journey on The Camino. I went back to the dormitory and recharged my phone before returning the charger plug to Cynthia at about 10:00 p.m. he had lent it to me days before and had said we would meet again, and I could return it then. I said goodnight and "Buen Camino," thanking the young woman for entrusting her phone charger to me. She seemed to be lost in another world. It was to be the last time I would encounter her on my Camino. She was still seeking answers, logically, answers to her own purpose for being, and I hoped and trusted she would continue her Camino to Santiago.

As I lay on my back in the dormitory of the Monastery of San Juan de Ortega, I recalled the pilgrim's blessing of the priest at the mass earlier in the evening:

"Oh God, you gifted your servant Abraham of the city of Ur of the Chaldeans, safety in all his pilgrimages, and you were the guide of the Jewish people through the desert. Please, through the intercession of San Juan de Ortega, with whose tomb we are, save the children of yours who, for the love of your name, make The Camino de Santiago! I ask for them on the road companionship, guidance at the crossroads, breath in fatigue, defence in danger, shelter along the way, a gentle breeze in heat, protection before the cold light in the darkness, consolation in disappointment and firmness in purpose, so that with your guidance they arrive unharmed at the end of their pilgrimage and enriched thanksgiving and virtues, return them safely to their homes full or perennial joy. We ask this through Christ the Lord. AMEN."

Then there was a prayer of guidance for the rest of the pilgrimage:

"May the Lord, through San Juan de Ortega, direct your steps and be favourable in inseparable companionship along the way. " And just to top it all off: "May the Holy Virgin Mary dispense her maternal protection, defend the dangers of soul and body, and under the mantle of Mother, may you deserve to arrive safely at the end of your pilgrimage. AMEN"

Then I rolled onto my side and saw many faces from the past before I fell into slumber and slept like a baby until the flashing of lights in the dead of night awoke me.

I was woken at 3:00 a.m. in the monastery dormitory by the clatter of Italian bike riders packing their gear for the day's ride. Torches and headlamps repeatedly swept across my eyes as they hurried to prepare, keen to set off in the dark before the heat made their journey unbearable. I reasoned that riding before dawn was probably safer for them anyway—with lights on their helmets and bikes alike. Strangely, their noise and impromptu light show came as a relief. They had interrupted a dark drinking dream, the kind that had visited me from time to time since giving up alcohol seven years earlier. In fact, that night's dream stood in sharp contrast to the one before it—a dream of a beautiful maiden. Like many of my Camino dreams, it made little sense to me.

Perhaps it was the monastery itself, or the lingering presence of the Pilgrim's Prayer spoken at the tomb of San Juan de Ortega in the adjoining chapel. And yet, if that were so, why the maiden? Why the drinking dreams? The Camino had a way of stirring both the sacred and the unresolved, often in the same breath. I never did get a proper night's sleep on the Camino. If it wasn't someone talking in their sleep, snoring, or farting inside a sleeping bag, it was Italian cyclists whispering urgently in the dark, flashing lights with complete oblivion to the pilgrims lying wide awake in the surrounding beds. If the Camino was teaching surrender by day, it was certainly testing it by night.

My diary recall the dreams I had nd the reason for mt eraly start that morning, as the next village was only about 3 km from the monastery, and it had been far too early to have breakfast; the next village after was 8 km further on made sense, so I had decided that would be a good goal to aim for to partake of my usual ritual breakfast. I read my diary entry, recalling how I quickly dressed in the dark, being careful not to make a sound, since it was quiet after the Italians' departure. Once my eyes adjusted to the dark outside, I could make out the shadowed silhouette of the chapel behind me and readied my walking poles for the task ahead. It had not occurred to me, the evening prior, to check for the Camino shell or yellow-arrowed directions to determine which way to take in the darkness. I realised that my headlamp and small hand torch were in the middle of my backpack and would be difficult to find in the darkness. I stood for a moment to consider my options: whether to go back to bed until there was enough light to see or to find the light in the monastery's registry office and find my headlamp and torch, or maybe just to hand over to whoever is running this show.

My dilemma was solved in an instant when, out of the darkness, a white robe appeared like a ghost in the night. It was the monk I always saw kneeling in prayer whenever I entered a chapel or church. The fact that his daily journeys began when the majority of pilgrims were still asleep or contemplating the day ahead in the comfort of their beds was also why he was always ahead of me, even on days when I walked fast. He quickly moved along the track ahead of me and appeared to know the exact way to traverse the darkness. The white robe was a beacon of light for me, so I quickly followed in his footsteps. Although I could now see the pathway beneath my feet, the monk's robe gave me added assurance.

I wasn't sure how long I could keep up with his pace, as he was so athletic and moved very quickly in the dark. I had not followed him for more than five minutes when he suddenly took a left turn onto another track; I followed in haste as he quickened his pace. No more than one hundred metres along the path, he suddenly stopped, about ten metres in front of me. I, too, stopped and waited for his next move as he raised his habit, turned his head towards me while facing his body away, and said, in English but with a Hungarian accent, "I am just taking a piss." He identified himself as Brother John of the Order of Mother Theresa. The spiritual endeavour was his sixth Camino, and he did it in the manner of the early Camino de Santiago pilgrims. He had completed each previous Camino without carrying any food, water or money. He apparently asked fellow pilgrims for food during the day, a custom of The Camino. In the evening, he approached restaurant owners for food. Sometimes they refused, but he overcame this by waiting until the owner had left the kitchen and then returning to approach the cook, who, in the owner's absence, gladly gave him food.

Being The Camino, sharing both food and clothing is commonplace among pilgrims, and water is never an issue as it's always in plentiful supply at the towns' and villages' central square fountains. Brother John's accommodation was usually in a monastery or albergue, where there was a request to place a coin in the donation box if one could afford it. Brother John asked me if I was Australian and where I lived. I told him about Sydney, and he mentioned the beauty of our harbour, the bridge and the Opera House. He had worked with some street kids and drug addicts in Kings Cross, stating that it was "a bad place."

Brother John had concluded that this was to be his last Camino, as he planned to return to Hungary for a year to teach at Budapest University before returning to the road to assist youth on the streets and people experiencing poverty. After some minutes together, he said he had to go on to pray and quickly increased his pace, leaving me to walk the Camino de Santiago by instinct. We met later in the day at an albergue in Burgos City. He gave me a prayer card with the Sacred Heart of Jesus on one side and a prayer in Hungarian on the reverse. He left me with a farewell: "Jesus is watching you and looking after you, Doug." I kept the prayer card, but I still have no idea what the Hungarian prayer says.

The Missionary of Charity is a Roman Catholic religious order established by Mother Theresa in 1950. Members take a vow of chastity, poverty, obedience, and a fourth vow, to give "…wholehearted free service to the poorest of the poor." In 1963, contemplative and active branches were founded. The Brother priesthood was established by an Australian Jesuit who became known as Brother Andrew. These missionaries care for refugees, ex-prostitutes, the mentally ill, sick and abandoned children, lepers and people with AIDS. They operate schools, educate street children and provide soup kitchens and many other services, without charge, for people irrespective of their religion or social status. As with the Sisters, the Priests, Brothers, lay Catholics and non-Catholics constituting Mother Theresa's co-workers live a simple life without television, radio or items of convenience, and neither drink alcohol nor smoke or beg for food. The influence of this order of Sisters and Brothers of the Order of Mother Theresa is a worldwide way of life for many.

He had long gone ahead of me, and in the dawning light, I could see the village of Ages, across the remote landscape, getting ever closer. I had travelled some four kilometres, and looked forward to an early breakfast – my usual orange juice, coffee and croissant. To the south, a slight detour would take me to the local church and a small bridge, attributed to San Juan de Ortega, across the **Rio Vena**, but I thought it was far too early to take in the sights, and all I wanted was food. As fate would have it, no café was open, so I resolved to walk on to **Atapuerca,** another 2.5 kilometres, which I calculated would take about 30 minutes, reassured by the knowledge that breakfast was not far away. I had climbed a rocky pathway not long after Brother John had quickened his pace and left me in his dust. I wondered how he managed to walk this rough track in his sandals, as I was having difficulty in boots.

My goal for the day was **Burgos**, some 23 kilometres away to the south. I had planned to climb the Sierra Atapuerca, visit the prehistoric ruins, stroll along the **Rio Arlanzon** and take in the marvellous architecture of the Burgos Cathedral. My village-to-village guidebook and topographic map showed the route to Burgos as quiet roads between quaint villages and peaceful dirt paths through pine forests, so I contented myself with the gentle pace of walking, despite the pain of my blistered feet. My mind drifted back to the previous night, in the monastery albergue, into the vision of my sleep, to that visit from an angelic maiden whose beauty and figure were beyond compare. She had danced across my mind, casting a spell of mystery and longing, the likes of which I had never known. As I walked the trail to Atapuerca, I wondered if she was some beauty who may have slept nearby in the albergue; if perhaps I had been half awake and had actually experienced a dancing maiden nearby albergue bunk in the dark. The dream had seemed so real, but I decided to put it out of my mind as I had done with the nightmare of my past alcoholic behaviour that had visited me on my rude awakening at 3:00 am, when the Italians had flashed their lights into my eyes while packing their bags for the day ahead.

I cast the dreams of the night before out of my mind as I sighted the café bar in Atapuerca nearby, and headed there for breakfast. Then after eating, I purchased another coffee and went to a table outside to sit in the early-morning sun and rest my still-blistered feet. I gazed down the track behind me, and to my amazement, the vision of pure beauty I had encountered in my dream the previous night was approaching the café, accompanied by a second stunning Spanish beauty.

With joy, like a small boy, I handed her my coffee and invited them both to sit with me. At the café bar I ordered two more coffees, one for the second beauty and one for myself. Although the Spanish embodiment of my dream did not speak English, her companion did, so we introduced ourselves and talked about our Camino experiences. Juana, my vision of pure beauty, was quite reserved at first but warmed to our conversation through her friend, Alexandra, who translated Spanish to English for me and acted as a go-between. We finished our coffee and agreed to walk together to Burgos, where this leg of the journey would end for them; they would return the following year to complete another leg. I did not ascertain where their journey had commenced this time, but they had been walking for a couple of weeks. It is common for European pilgrims to do a couple of weeks every year until they have completed the entire 800 km trek to Santiago. Some pilgrims take up to ten years to complete the walk, returning year after year until the task is done and the Compostela certificate is attained. It takes a madman like me to attempt the whole thing in one go.

To be fair, those of us who live down under have a long distance to travel to get to Spain, and the flights are expensive, so we like to make the most of it. At least that is what I told myself, even though I had an agenda: to release my stored-up burdens from my life's experiences and to search for a symbolic but imaginary Sword of Discernment. Perhaps, I considered, the symbol I sought was in the shape of my previous night's dream – the beauty who now walked beside me, as we headed along the track south to Burgos, like three amigos on The Way.

Tinker Bell did come to me then, almost like a dream made flesh. Not as a fantasy to be chased, nor an illusion dancing just out of reach, but as someone fully present, here with me in the moment. There was no promise beyond the day we shared, and strangely, that was enough. I had learned by then that not all encounters are meant to be held—some are meant only to be recognised.

Chapter 8. Like ships in the night.

What we shared lasted but a single day on **The Way**, yet it carried a lightness that did not fade with distance. There was no grasping, no longing to make it more than it was. Just conversation, laughter, and the quiet knowing that, despite future distance, we would not part; we would always remain friends.

We joked, laughed and danced, held hands, and sang our way south, in the heat of the Spanish summer's day. The constant pounding of our feet on the hard surface of the highway and byways of The Way played havoc with our blistered feet. The women were suffering just as much as I was, and my Spanish beauty appeared to suffer even more. I noticed that she occasionally had tears in her eyes, and I wondered whether this was due to past-life pain she was re-experiencing on this leg of The Camino, or because their mutual journey for this year was about to end in Burgos.

At the time, in the company of the two angels of the road, my journey seemed more straightforward, and my backpack felt lighter, although the constant needles of torture in my feet did not ease. Juana had talked to me through her companion, speaking of her loss of a husband after six years of marriage and the cancer that had almost taken the life of one of her two sons when he was a young boy. He had somehow beaten the disease and was now a fit and healthy young man. From the photo she showed me on her iPhone, I judged the boys to be in their mid-twenties and, although single, they were happy. Her husband had died some twenty-two years ago, and she had raised the boys by herself. Our now mutual friend, Alexandra, helped me complete the picture of Juana's life. She had close family ties and loved dancing and listening to her favourite classical music – including Beethoven and The Three Tenors – which I also enjoyed in my quieter moments. However, at heart, I was still a child of rock 'n' roll and middle-of-the-road country music.

Juana, it seemed, loved to drive fast on the open roads, and her work routine, administering health products and advising women on health, took her on a daily 300 km round trip. Her husband had died many years ago while riding a motorbike, but that did not deter her from driving fast and letting her hair down. She loved to listen to music while driving between her home city of Valencia and the surrounding towns and villages.

She was a medical professional, specialising in diet and exercise for middle-aged women; judging by her figure, she was a perfect specimen for her clientele. She reminded me of the smooth lines of a Porsche sports car herself-stylish, smooth, sexier than other models and ready for action.

On the Camino, we meet people the way ships pass in the night—briefly, often without knowing their names, their stories brushing against ours for a moment before disappearing again. Some disturb our sleep, some share a meal, some walk beside us for a few hours or a few days. Rarely do they stay. Yet each encounter seems to serve a purpose. Sometimes they are there to test our patience, sometimes to lighten the load with laughter, and sometimes simply to remind us that we are not walking alone, even when the journey feels solitary. We may never understand why a particular soul crosses our path, but often their presence prepares us for the next stage of the road.

It's pretty amazing how people openly tell perfect strangers about their life, love, pain of loss, and sorrow while on The Camino. Juana was no exception, and I'm sure that if I had pried Alexandra for her story, she would have similarly responded. I recalled my journey to date and noted that I had shared and cried over the loss of my son Peter on a couple of occasions during this cathartic inward journey. Such displays were emotional, nothing new on The Camino de Santiago, as pilgrims since Medieval times had taken the inward journey, shared their life woes, made sacrifices and offerings, and let go of their material and emotional burdens. However, right then and there, I was more interested in enjoying the company of my fellow pilgrims and resolved not to think too much about the past for the remainder of the day. We stopped for lunch in the quiet little town of **Cardenuela de Riopico** before continuing along peaceful paved roads through Orbaneja, about one kilometre away, where the road split. We had already walked some 14 km, and during lunch, another weary pilgrim advised that we could leave the yellow markings along the well-worn highway to Burgos and instead take the unmarked, less-travelled road.

This alternate route crossed the **Rio Arlandzon** and followed the river on a peaceful, shady, easy-to-navigate dirt track, even though it was unmarked. I was in favour of taking this detour, but the diversion involved a longer walk into Burgos City, so I went along with my Spanish companions' decision, and we followed the busy highway route, a distance of 13.5 km. It did not seem a wise choice, as far as I was concerned, and it proved to be the wrong route, as there was no shade and the sun poured down on the hot pavement, making every step unbearable. At one point, Juana stopped and quietly cried, but we encouraged her to go on despite the pain she was experiencing from her blisters and sore feet. I resolved to encourage the women to keep on track, and that took my mind off my own pain. The final 10 km were the most difficult, as we entered the city through the industrial area where there was no relief from the passing trucks and cars on this busy, noisy stretch of road. We were about 5 km from the city centre when my left ankle gave way, with a lot of pain, and my swollen feet made things even worse. I decided to say goodbye to the Spanish beauties who, like me, were in no mood for conversation by then and only wanted to find an albergue and rest.

I sat on the concrete at the edge of the road and ate the last piece of the fruit I had purchased in one of the villages along the route and watched the mirage of my day on the road – the two Spanish beauties – slowly fade into the distance. I had only 500 mm of water left, but knew it was enough to see me through until I reached a bar or café on the city's outskirts. I entered a shopping strip on the poor side of the town, by the side of the busy highway. Blocks of residential apartments surrounded the shops. I found my way to an electronics store to see if I could purchase a phone charger compatible with my iPhone. I did find a suitable charger plug in a small convenience store. I also spotted a yellow arrow on a building; it led me to the city centre and the cathedral, its inner sanctum a sharp contrast to the noisy, poor outer-city area from which I had emerged. The cathedral was the central feature of a magnificent ancient city filled with historic art and architecture, which I had read about in my travel guide.

Finding an albergue only a stone's throw from the cathedral in the heart of the city was not difficult, as the yellow arrows on buildings were always prominent. The Albergue was a relatively new building, surrounded by a famous food court, the Spanish delights of which had won national food awards. I made my way to the busy register counter, where many pilgrims were seeking accommodation for the night. I noted that the complex contained several floors, and I was sure I would have a bed for the night. It was like a modern hotel, and after registration and the stamping of my pilgrim's passport, I took the lift to my designated room and bed on the third floor, where I found, along a corridor, a private dormitory containing eight bunks. Fate is fortune, as who should be occupying the first two bunks? None other than my fateful Spanish beauties, my companions of the road!

I had a shower and used the large bench area to clean and dress my blistered feet and secure a stretch bandage around my swollen ankle for support. Back in the dormitory, I was greeted by Juana, seated on her bunk and in great distress, having difficulty with her wounded feet. I sat next to her in silence and began to dress her blisters and massaged her feet with the sweet-smelling liniment I had purchased from a chemist's store a day or two before. She put her pretty head on my shoulder and cried like a child. Once both girls had recouped energy after a brief rest, they went off to dinner together. I declined their offer to join them, preferring instead to meet up with some fellow pilgrims with whom I had walked during days past.

One of those pilgrims was Raimon, my crazy French friend of The Way. The others were a band of excited young people I had encountered earlier. We headed to a nearby bar and joined yet other pilgrims, exchanging stories of our individual Caminos. My mind still sensed the scent of a woman, and my fingers still retained the odour of the liniment. Raimon must have sensed my distracted state of mind and seemed to grasp the essence of my thoughts, even my desire to fulfil the mythical nonsense of my symbolic need to find a sword representing my inner warrior.

The Spanish beauty loomed strongly in my mind as a distraction from my journey and the real purpose of my Camino. As if attuned to my inner wondering, Raimon suddenly produced some blue balloons from his trouser pocket and inflated them, with laughter from those surrounding him. He looked at me with a smile, similar to his smile when he had found the four-leaf clover the previous day, and quickly fashioned a sword with a handle, much like my vision of a sword I had described to him in a dream– except that it was blue, not red like in my dream. In recall now it had been a symbolic sword of my inner need of a type of Templar symbolism, or that of a sword of one whose heart had been wounded by sorrow, or had it been like that of Sir Thomas Moore who had mornfully stated: "And the heart that is soonest awake to the flowers is always the first to be touch'd by the thorns."

Perhaps it was his way of telling me to stick to my dream and my imagination and not become distracted again. He asked a passing pilgrim to take a photo of us together, with him holding the balloon sword aloft. I closed my eyes and asked the God of Brother, John of the Order of Mother Theresa, for guidance, in a meditative stance of respect for the young man. I thought for a moment that Raimon's balloon sword could just be a sign from God of my inner power, a sign from St. James, or of the Templar Knights or just a lot of hot air. My logical mind told me it was just hot air, but I had great faith in my imagination and chose to hold on to my goal for now. Another quote entered my mind as I smiled at the camera:

" The pen is mightier than the sword." In time, this was to come to pass, but I did not know it then as I do now.

I left my companions early in the evening as they settled into a drinking session and went off to investigate the inner city. I had a brief walk around the shops and noticed a nice-looking outdoor restaurant with a covered balcony where I could shelter from the still-hot evening sun. I found a seat with a good view of the street, ate an enjoyable meal and watched the passing parade of mainly Spanish families out for a stroll around the city's shops while waiting for the day to turn to dusk and the night to cool. After my meal, I made my way back to the cathedral for a last look inside before returning to the Albergue. The two Spanish beauties were asleep in their bunks, and I decided to get an early night's sleep too. I read a little from my hiking guide, looking for the route south out of the city, before realising that the yellow arrows I had found before venturing back to the Albergue would be adequate to have me back on the pathway to my ultimate destination. So, I switched off the bunk lamp and drifted into a deep, dreamless sleep. I awoke early and decided to go for an early-morning trek before the heat of the day set in.

Passing the bed of my sleeping Spanish dream, I ruffled her hair; she turned over to face me, and her outstretched hand squeezed mine. With a sleepy smile, she said, "Buen Camino", turned to her side and returned to slumber land. I thought of our previous day together on the road – our laughter, singing and hand-holding. It was true that my heart had been taken briefly by this dark beauty, but I knew that it was nothing but a passing fantasy. I wondered for a moment whether I should have taken the route to Burgos via the river, rather than venturing on with the two women. I realised that if I had made the logical choice, I would not now be suffering the hollow ache in my heart. My mind became distracted by the many wounds that I carried, resulting from a broken heart, and I remembered the biblical story of Mary's visit to a synagogue, where an old prophet told her, "Thy own soul a sword shall pierce." I was in search of a relic of sorts- a Sword of Discernment, insight into a symbolic reality that I could somehow hold on to. Here I was, in my imagination, but in fact with one additional notch in the dagger within my heart.

Putting all thoughts out of my mind, I headed for the nearest café for my usual breakfast of freshly squeezed orange juice, croissant and coffee before once again continuing on the road. There, I contemplated the confusion in my head and the feeling in my heart. "There is no fool like an old fool", I thought. The Spanish beauty was nothing more than a temporary distraction of the mind on a hot August day on my Camino – a way of relieving the burden of my soul and of keeping my thoughts away from the pain in my feet and the ever-present weight of unneeded burdens in my backpack. Reality had dawned, as plainly as day follows night. I resolved then and there not to allow any more angels of the road to distract me from the inner journey that I was coming to terms with. A determination that, in a future reality, did not prove to
be true.

It was not until the next evening that I came across a note in my backpack written in Spanish. It was from the Spanish beauty, "Thank you for your kindness to me on such a difficult day. I kiss you." If she had only known the intent of my heart at the time, she might not have written such heartfelt words.

I came to see that nothing on the Camino was accidental—not the noise in the night, not the fleeting conversations, not even the interruptions that left me tired and irritable by morning. Each was a lesson, quietly offered, helping to shape whatever lay ahead on the Way. And so, when dawn came, I shouldered my pack once more, carrying not only my fatigue but the subtle gifts left behind by those who had passed through my night.

As I reread the diary entries from that first Camino, I can see how often this pattern repeated itself. People appeared and disappeared with little warning. Some walked with me for only a few kilometres, others for a single conversation or a shared meal. A few stayed longer, long enough to leave a mark. Some spoke openly of their pain, unburdening themselves to a stranger they would never see again. Others offered laughter, stories, or simple companionship when the road grew long and silent. Some challenged me, unknowingly pressing against my fears, my impatience, or my attachments. At the time, I often dismissed these encounters as incidental. Looking back now, I can see they were anything but.

Each person carried a lesson I needed, even if I didn't recognise it at the time. One taught me endurance by walking on in silence. Another taught me humility by accepting help without explanation. Some reflected parts of myself I would rather not have seen, while others showed me glimpses of who I might yet become. The Camino had a way of assigning teachers without asking for my consent.

What strikes me most, reading those pages now, is how rarely these encounters were about comfort. More often, they unsettled me, disrupted my routines, or forced me to confront something unresolved. And yet, each disruption prepared me —quietly, steadily—for what lay ahead. Not just the next village or mountain pass, but the deeper terrain I would have to cross within myself. In this way, the Camino was never merely a physical journey. It was a procession of encounters, each timed perfectly, each arriving and departing before I could cling too tightly. I was learning, step by step, that the purpose of these fleeting meetings was not attachment, but transformation.

And as I turned the pages of that old diary, I realised something else: the road had been guiding me all along, not just through landscapes and villages, but through people—each one a messenger, helping me prepare for the next stage of the Way. Each person carried a lesson I needed, even if I didn't recognise it at the time. One taught me endurance by walking on in silence. Another taught me humility by accepting help without explanation. Some reflected parts of myself I would rather not have seen, while others showed me glimpses of who I might yet become. The Camino had a way of assigning teachers without asking for my consent. What strikes me most, reading those pages now, is how rarely these encounters were about comfort. More often, they unsettled me, disrupted my routines, or forced me to confront something unresolved. And yet, each disruption prepared me —quietly, steadily—for what lay ahead. Not just the next village or mountain pass, but the deeper terrain I would have to cross within myself. In this way, the Camino was never merely a physical journey. It was a procession of encounters, each timed perfectly, each arriving and departing before I could cling too tightly. I was learning, step by step, that the purpose of these fleeting meetings was not attachment, but transformation. And as I turned the pages of that old diary, I realised something else: the road had been guiding me all along, not just through landscapes and villages, but through people—each one a messenger, helping me prepare for the next stage of the Way.

Chapter 9. On the road again.

The dream of the Spanish beauty stayed with me. For that one day we walked together, what formed was not romance but a friendship that would endure—a pen-pal connection carried across languages through the kindness of a translator and the patience of shared curiosity. It was gentle, respectful, and honest in a way that needed no more than it was.

Then there was another — an English beauty — who walked with me for only a short while, yet stayed with me through the years. Even now, when I reflect, I hear her constant refrain whenever something unfolded in a strangely perfect or miraculous way: *"Well, that's the Camino."* She seemed to sense we would meet again, yet we did not cross paths in Santiago. Or so I thought.

When I arrived at the Cathedral for the pilgrim's Mass, there were no seats left. As I stood there, resigned to missing the celebration, I suddenly heard her voice call out, "Doug, I've saved a seat for you." In that moment, her words rang true once more. That quiet time together became another ship passing in the night—a shared lesson, a shared grace—and then we both moved on.

There were so many encounters like that: moments filled with laughter, singing, shared meals, and sometimes tears. Each one is brief, yet somehow complete in itself. Among the most memorable were the days I spent walking with a band of young brothers. They spoke openly of troubles they had encountered early in life—lessons they were already learning, while I was only just beginning to face similar truths myself. We walked, ate, talked, and laughed together. I admired their carefree spirit, though I came to see that they, too, carried burdens. They were on a rite of passage into adulthood; I was an older pilgrim learning how to let go of what had weighed me down for decades. One of those young men was a rock musician. It was his presence and his curiosity about a poem I had written that quietly turned something within me. He wanted to turn that poem into a song. That simple exchange—unplanned, unforced—became a turning point. It rekindled something creative in me that continues to influence my life to this day.

Looking back now, I see how each of these encounters arrived precisely when needed, then moved on without explanation. Ships in the night, each carrying a lesson, each helping me toward the next stage of my journey—whether I understood it at the time or not. That, too, was the Camino.

I was paused in thought of the notes in my diary, noting the entry as **Burgos to Sahagun**: " …leaving the majestic city of Burgos, thinking back to the entry in the medieval grandeur and the promenade of the banks of the Duern and Arlanza rivers, entering the peaceful wasteland of the Meseta, walking among immense crop fields, through small villages."

Then another diary note "Entering the Medieval stronghold of **Homiles del Camino** [accompanied with photos from my iPhone]… the peaceful wasteland of **the Mesata** before the gradual climb up the plateau and the descent to the river Bol woods. The gradual climb and the descent into the valley of the river Bol woods and the holm oaks. The natural track follows along the old Roman road with its original paved surfaces." I had many a note throughout my diary like this, notes typical of a tourist view for later recall. However, it was not the ancient architecture nor that history that fascinated me; it was the story of The Way and my fellow pilgrims that captured my attention:

Negotiating the long, winding route through the maze of streets leading out of Burgos would have been almost impossible without the yellow arrows pointing the way south. Though they deface the walls of ancient buildings in cities, towns, and villages along the Camino, these roughly painted arrows are regarded as almost sacred. They are accepted—even protected—by municipal councils, for they have become enduring symbols of the Way itself.

I shared a coffee break with a young Belgian pilgrim as we took a final salute to the magnificent city of Burgos, with its immeasurable architectural wealth and historic art—a place steeped in myth and legend. Like me, he had seen enough culture for one day. We were both eager to leave the city behind and regain the quieter, more mystical rhythm of walking our own paths, each in our own space. It was the freedom of nature and the youth, and the lessons of acceptance that I learnt from them, that fascinated me.

I noted a diary entry for future reference: "We shared a final laugh when he noticed a pretty South African girl passing by, wearing his favourite top. He had left it behind in the albergue while packing his knapsack. With a grin, he remarked that it looked better on her than it ever had on him, and so he let her walk on without saying a word."

In that small moment, I saw how easily we were learning to let go. Possessions, pride, even small attachments no longer mattered. The Camino was quietly loosening the grip of the false self, teaching us that what we carry inside is far more critical than what we leave behind. And with that understanding, we turned south once more, surrendered to the mystic madness of the Way.

I left the city behind for a peaceful, flat, and unchanging landscape. I chose no car, no bus, no bicycle, no horse. I walked, carrying everything I owned on my back. Many of us had begun this way, intent on completing the Camino as it had always been walked.

As I reached the edge of Burgos, the sound of church bells faded into the distance. Each step onto the Meseta was painful and deliberate. I knew for whom the bells tolled. They tolled for what I was leaving behind, and for what I had not yet become. It would take more than one Camino to become what I was destined to be, but I didn't know it then as I do now.

Beyond the city, the Meseta opened into silence. A vast, unyielding stillness that offered little distraction and no shelter from one's own thoughts. I walked into it carrying not only my pack, but the inner resistance and doubt that such a landscape inevitably awakens. There was nowhere to hide from them here.

This vast plain has tested pilgrims for centuries—saints and sinners, kings and confessors alike—stripping each traveller of illusion as surely as it strips the land of excess. In medieval times, as now, it demanded patience, endurance, and faith without ornament. It asked the same questions of every soul who crossed it.

With each measured step, the Camino grew quieter, and so did I. And in that silence, I began to understand that the Meseta was not empty at all. It was a place where the noise of the world fell away, leaving only what truly mattered to be faced.

Looking back now, I did not know then that I would walk the Meseta again some five years later—worn down, weathered, and having once more fallen into despair and regret. That return would not be under the heat of the desert sun, but in cold, freezing rain, through a quagmire of mud and slush.

Another lesson awaited me there. It became clear that on the road to spiritual destiny, many landscapes must be crossed—both outer and inner—and each frontier demands its own endurance. I was reminded once again- The Way does not repeat itself for comfort, but for learning. What I could not see then was that the Camino would call me back, not to punish me, but to deepen what I had not yet fully understood.

Honduras, my intended destination for the day, lay across the desert wasteland beneath the relentless Spanish summer sun, and for me it proved a bridge too far. I did, however, make it as far as Hornillos del Camino, some eleven kilometres short of my goal. By late afternoon, the constant pounding of my feet on the hot, dry, unforgiving surface of the Way had taken its toll.

I decided to stay in what appeared to be the only Albergue in the small village, where I could soak and tend to my blistered feet. I was also drawn by the promise of a pilgrim's meal, advertised on a rough tin sign at the roadside near the village entrance—a simple invitation, but a welcome one. The spring fountain of **San Bol** lay just six kilometres ahead, with Hontanas another five beyond that. A night of rest, followed by a gentler walk south in the morning, seemed the wisest course. And it was. I was given a single room and a generous three-course meal. Fresh salad, veal, and a curd dessert—washed down with a couple of alcohol-free beers—followed by an early night's sleep, proved to be precisely what I needed.

I rose before dawn, the village still wrapped in silence. **Hornillos del Camino** lay hushed beneath a pale sky, as if holding its breath. My feet were tender but calmer, soothed by rest and care, and my pack felt lighter—not because it weighed less, but because I had learned, if only briefly, how to carry it.

I walked out of the village alone, the road stretching ahead in a long, narrow line toward San Bol. There were no bells this morning, no voices, only the steady rhythm of my steps and the soft breath of the land waking around me. In that silence, I felt ready once more—not to conquer the Way, but to walk with it. The Camino does not hurry those who listen.

 I begin to dig deeper into my old diary notes:

"This old man had crossed the desert wasteland and reached another oasis—an ancient village blessed with many springs and abundant water. Along the way, I had been warned of dangerous wild wolves said to hunt in packs around the villages. They were believed to lie hidden in the valley of a small river, unseen until it was too late. Legend had it that they roamed the village at night, attacking sheep and, on occasion, even humans."

Because of this, my fellow pilgrims and I were advised that it was safest to cross the river and the surrounding desert in the middle of the day, when dogs guarded the sheep—dogs said to be anything but ferocious. I took these warnings with a grain of salt, filing them away as yet another myth or piece of Camino folklore, not unlike my imagined Sword of Discernment. I found myself smiling inwardly at the stories. For what would become my first book was, unknowingly, in its embryonic stage, curled up like a seed about to flower within.

I was not afraid of dogs, wild or otherwise. As for river crossings, I had been born near a coastal river and the open sea. I had swum where sharks were an ever-present possibility, walked barefoot where red-bellied black snakes lay hidden, and endured bites and stings from poisonous ticks, spiders, and bees. Compared to that, a river crossing and a few wolves of legend did not trouble me in the least. The Camino, it seemed, was once again offering stories to measure against experience—and quietly inviting me to decide which fears truly deserved my attention.

My dirty boots, caked with the dust of the **Meseta**, had me reviewing the lessons learned to this point on the Camino. Outwardly, I had little fear of what nature might place before me. I was not afraid of man or beast, of heat or distance, of hunger or discomfort. These were known trials—visible, tangible, and somehow honest. What unsettled me lay deeper.

Beneath the steady rhythm of my walking, another terrain was revealing itself: an inner depth of feeling I had not yet fully confronted. There, in the shadowed well of self-doubt, the dragon waited—its mouth coiled like a serpent, silent but watchful. It was not a creature of sudden attack, but of slow erosion, whispering questions of worth, acceptance, and surrender.

The inner seed of my being was the true frontier that required my attention. Not courage of the body, but courage of the soul. Acceptance—not as resignation, but as a willingness to remain present with what arose. I sensed that this inner work could not be forced, nor outrun. It would come, as the Camino so often does, in a way not yet expected—quietly, insistently, and at precisely the moment I believed myself prepared.

The Way was not finished with me yet.

Continuing my journey, I dismissed any lingering fears of danger in the natural world. The thought of encountering a wild wolf seemed remote, almost theatrical, and I shrugged it away with the growing awareness that nature, like life itself, holds both cruelty and kindness in equal measure. In this vast desert country, I saw neither sheep nor wolves—only the silence. I guessed the predators had long vanished, perhaps even before the village's fourteenth-century protective walls began their slow surrender to time.

I knew I had ample time that morning to tend to myself, so after breakfast I wandered briefly through the village and purchased more Band-Aids and a small jar of sweet-smelling ointment. Its lid bore the familiar image of a Camino pilgrim and the scallop shell, a quiet reassurance stamped in tin. I applied the *"Urgent Traditional Mundi Camino"* cream to my swollen ankle and blistered feet, carefully dressing my wounds before pulling on a clean pair of socks.
I assumed the instructions said something along the lines of *traditional urgent treatment for the journey*. I recognised petroleum jelly and Aloe Vera among the ingredients; the rest, written in Spanish, remained a mystery—though by now I had learned that faith often works just as well without translation.

As I tightly laced my boots, I recognised a small but meaningful ritual in the act. Each knot felt like a renewed commitment—to keep walking, to trust the process, and to accept whatever lessons lay ahead. With that, I stepped back onto the Camino, carrying not only my pack, but a growing awareness that healing, like the journey itself, happens one deliberate step at a time.

It had always been a hidden quest in my life, like that of a warrior on a mission, or a seeker in search of the Grail. Following the road less travelled was simply in my nature. I had never fitted comfortably within well-worn paths or predictable lives. I trusted the call of the unknown more than the promise of safety. That was until the wound was driven deep—right into my core.

I lost everything that had once defined me: my family, my friends, my career, my sense of belonging, even my desire to keep living. One by one, the outer structures collapsed until there was nothing left to hold me upright. I sank into the desolate places of despair, depression, and anguish—those inner wastelands where time stands still and hope feels like a foreign language. I did not fall all at once. It was a slow unravelling—a quiet erosion of faith in myself and in life. I wandered there for a long time, stripped of identity, stripped of purpose, carrying a grief I could neither explain nor escape. The warrior was gone, the quest forgotten. All that remained was survival.

It seems now that God was calling me even then, in my darkest hour. Blinded by the depth of despair, I so often turned toward women for comfort, instead of turning inward— toward the One within who alone could lead me from darkness into light. I searched for salvation in reflection rather than in the source.

For much of my life, I had been like Peter Pan, endlessly chasing Tinker Bell—always just out of reach, her beauty captivating, her light flickering on my endless Neverland journey. I travelled with my own band of lost boys, seeking a mythical sign born of imagination rather than truth. And whenever I managed to hold a woman close, to believe I had found the Grail, it revealed itself as something fragile and artificial—a cup that crumbled into nothingness in my hands.

Yet the Camino, I came to understand, was leading me elsewhere. It was not a path toward another, but a path inward—toward the man who had always been there, waiting. The real warrior. The one who did not flee from silence, nor hide behind longing.

For it was true: I had to enter the depths of the dragon's mouth before reality could lead me into the light. Only by facing that darkness could the fire be transformed—not into destruction, but into creation. Out of that crucible would come the true expression of my creative self, not for escape, but for the benefit of others.

And there, beyond the dragon's breath, were the soothing waters—waters that began to heal my sorrowful self, to cleanse my wounded soul, and to restore purpose, not in fantasy, but in deed. I had spent a lifetime, it seemed, tilting at windmills, lady loves, business interests and embarking on many quests, both mental and spiritual. The thought depressed me a little, as here I was, once again on another quest to find a symbolic representation of a mythical Sword of Discernment. I forced myself to lift my spirits and laugh at my foolishness and the notion of finding some silly sword awaiting me in **Santiago** at the end of my journey. Yes, it was true, I thought once more – there is no fool like an old fool, and gave that thought some worth by calling out, "Boys will always be boys". Of course, here in hindsight, in the now, as I searched for meaning in those diary entries, there was a creative grail of sorts, but it would not come to me until the time was ripe for future revelation.

I stepped back onto The Way. The yellow arrow pointed forward, as it always did—unconcerned with my revelations, unmoved by my metaphors, indifferent to whether I had just slain a dragon or merely changed my socks. The Camino, in its quiet wisdom, rarely applauds inner breakthroughs. It simply says: *walk*.

The Meseta stretched ahead, flat and honest, offering nowhere to hide. No forests for mystery, no mountains for drama—just sky, dust, and the steady rhythm of breath and footfall. It was the sort of landscape that had undone saints and sinners alike, not by confrontation but by repetition. Step after step, thought after thought, until resistance softened and the noise within grew tired of its own voice.

Out here, theology did not need words. Blisters preached their own sermons. Hunger rang clearer than church bells. And silence—true silence—became both companion and teacher. I found myself walking not *toward* answers, but *with* them, letting them rise and fall like the land itself. Now and then, another pilgrim would appear on the horizon, approach, exchange a few words, perhaps a laugh, and then drift away again—ships passing quietly in daylight this time. No grand confessions, no shared epiphanies. Just the unspoken recognition that we were all carrying something, and that walking was how we learned to loosen our grip on it. The dragon had not vanished. He simply learned to walk beside me, shrinking with each kilometre.

And Peter Pan, if he was still around, had finally taken off his wings, discovering that it was the ground beneath his feet—not the sky—that was teaching him how to grow.

Chapter 10. New garment from old cloth.

So I walked on, across the ancient spine of Spain, one yellow guiding arrow at a time—no longer chasing the Grail, no longer running from the fire—just moving forward, step by step, into the reality of the road to whatever awaited beyond the next horizon. And in that knowing, the boy finally stepped aside, making room for the man who could walk on without regret.

A brief rest just outside the village of **Castrojeriz** was another necessary pause in the journey for me. I removed my boots and socks and soaked my fiery feet in a stream. A young man and his girlfriend sat down with me and copied my actions.

As we sat there talking, a feather drifted down from the heavens above and came to rest at our feet. The three of us looked up into the vast blue sky, but there was no bird in sight—no winged culprit to claim it. It felt like a slight wink from the Camino, the sort of thing you stop questioning after a while. Moments like this were not unusual on The Way. In fact, they seemed to multiply the further I walked, as though coincidence itself had decided to join the pilgrimage. Stranger happenings were still to come, though at the time I had no way of knowing that.

There we were—three pilgrims, strangers only moments earlier—sitting with our tired feet in the cool stream beside the path, sharing stories and silence in equal measure. And then this feather, arriving unannounced, as if nature itself had paused to join the conversation. "Birds of a feather flock together," I thought, smiling inwardly. Or perhaps it was simply the Camino reminding us that even brief gatherings have meaning, and that sometimes the message arrives without explanation, asking only to be noticed.

It was in these small snippets of memory that I found myself again, gathered from old diary entries written more than a decade earlier, memories for my present state of being in mindfulness. Turned another page of my diary:

" I arrived at Castrojeriz early in the afternoon and calculated that I had walked 21 km during the day. Considering the state of my feet and the many rest stops to treat them, I thought I had done well to get as far as I had. The next day was to be a 19km walk to Boadilla del Camino, and normally would have been an easy day for me, but with a backpack still weighing me down, and foot problems, a good rest before tackling the next leg of the journey made a lot of sense."

There were so many moments of recall—peaks and valleys of emotion—some gentle, others confronting. Reading them now, I could feel how close the inner journey had always been to the physical one, how quickly reflection gave way to raw reality. The hill proved especially steep after leaving the desert plain, rising sharply into the heat of midday sun. My backpack, familiar yet unforgiving, pressed heavily into my shoulders, while my feet—still swollen and blistered—made each step slower and more deliberate than I had anticipated.

There was no poetry in the climb, only effort. I moved upward steadily, if not gracefully, drawing quiet strength from the small supply of food tucked into my pack. It wasn't much, but it was enough. As was often the case on The Camino, it wasn't abundance that carried me forward—just what I needed, and no more.

I made it to the top of the mountain and, with relief, dropped my backpack onto a bench where other pilgrims sat in their own pockets of silence and exhaustion after the steep climb. No one spoke much. We didn't need to. The shared effort had said enough. Nearby, a table had been set with food and drink for pilgrims. An enterprising Spanish trader had hauled supplies up the mountain in an old van parked close by. There were no prices displayed. Instead, a simple sign read: *"Purchase by donation."* He had likely worked out that generosity would serve him better than fixed prices. After such a demanding ascent, every pilgrim was in genuine need of food and water, and gratitude loosens the purse more easily than obligation. Either way, his timing was perfect, and his presence felt almost providential.

He had even erected umbrellas over the benches to offer shade and comfort while we rested. It was a small kindness, but on The Camino, small kindnesses often arrived exactly when they were needed most.

I was back there again, if only for a moment, in a similar state of mind—though more worn now by life's accumulations. I sat in my present surroundings, my home cave, looking out at trees and listening to the sound of silence, just as I had after that climb to the top of the steep hill. It had been a shorter distance than the ascent of the Pyrenees, but far harder in the midday heat. I recalled not only the rest at the summit, but the small, unguarded conversations shared with fellow pilgrims on The Way. Each of us carried an inner journey we were still trying to make sense of—unfinished business, a quiet hope, a future imagined but not yet named. I hadn't realised it then. What felt like a single act of letting go was, in truth, the beginning of a pattern I would repeat on two more Camino journeys over the next five years.

Back then, on that high mountain ridge, we were simply passing time together—resting, eating, exchanging a few words—perhaps never to meet again in this lifetime. And yet, people you meet on the Camino never really leave you.

I remembered how, during a later depressive episode, I posted a message on Facebook saying I planned to walk the Camino for a third time in the coming months. Within twenty-four hours, twenty-seven pilgrims I had met on that first Camino in 2013 responded with messages of encouragement and the same familiar blessing: *Buen Camino.*

It reminded me that the Camino does not end at Santiago, nor even on the trail itself. It continues quietly, carried forward in memory, in connection, and in the unseen threads that bind strangers together long after the walking is done. Those messages faded back into memory, and with them the comfort of knowing I had not walked alone, even when I thought I had. The Camino has a way of reminding you of that—just when you are tempted to believe the journey is only yours to bear.

The rest at the summit did its quiet work. Bodies stirred, packs were shouldered once more, and one by one we rose from the benches, drawn back to the road as naturally as breath returning after effort. There was no announcement, no shared plan—just the unspoken understanding that it was time to walk again. I tightened my laces, adjusted the straps of my pack, and stepped back onto The Way. The path descended now, stretching ahead into the heat and distance, carrying me onward toward the next village, the subsequent encounter, the next lesson waiting to reveal itself—only in its own time.

The Camino always moves forward, whether you are ready or not.

My days had settled into a simple rhythm by then. An early breakfast stop at a café along the route for what I came to think of as my *Spanish breakfast*: a banana on toast, followed by coffee and a glass of cold water. A brief exchange of pleasantries with the proprietor—*"Muchas gracias, amigo"*—

and then a page or two written about the previous day's journey, before it slipped from my conscious mind. Sometimes I added a short note to myself, often about the quiet reward of compassion over judgment, tucked away as a footnote.

I was back on The Way by around eight in the morning, having travelled sections of the **Canal de Castilla** and followed what felt like the road less travelled—a happy wanderer at the time—tramping on foot from **Villalcázar** to **Carrión de los Condes.** The heat of the road still took some getting used to, but I was now enjoying the ease of meeting fellow pilgrims along the way, and time seemed to pass almost unnoticed. I arrived in Carrión de los Condes in the mid-afternoon.

As was my custom, I visited the local church, found a *refugio* —a hostel reserved specifically for pilgrims—prepared myself for the night, showered, washed the day's clothing, and then returned to the church. There, in the narthex, I joined a gathering of young people singing in unison with the nuns of Carrión de los Condes.

The narthex fascinated me. It was an area inside the church, yet separated from the nave—the "body" of the church —by a screen. I had noted in my diary that in modern times, the narthex simply means an entry or foyer. Still, initially, it was a place for those seeking penance for wrongdoing or those being instructed in the Christian faith. These people were not permitted to enter the nave until reconciliation or baptism had taken place.

The simplicity of the Spanish Catholic churches I visited always revealed the influence of many foreign powers, layered over centuries of destruction and rebuilding. In some cases, decay had demanded replacement; in others, the cost of rebuilding had stripped away former architectural symbolism. And yet, Catholic vision traditionally assigns meaning to almost everything within a church: the roof symbolising charity, the floor, the foundation of faith, and the humanity of people with low incomes, the columns, the apostles, priests, and bishops—those who bear the weight of human infirmity toward heavenly bliss, The beams, the champions of ecclesiastical right, defenders of faith even unto death. The nave—the body—symbolised Noah's Ark and the Barque of St Peter, outside of which no one is saved.

There were many more symbols I had written about then. Looking back now, I realise I no longer stood as firmly in my commitment to my Christian upbringing. Yet I view it all with a solemn intrigue. Some inner progress had been made, but my outward expression of faith had retreated into quieter shadows compared to those days when I stood among the youth, singing in that candle-lit chapel entrance—half inside, half outside—lingering on the threshold.

Where once I sang effortlessly at the threshold of the church, now I linger there differently—less convinced, more contemplative. Not outside in rejection, but not fully inside either. The narthex, once an architectural curiosity, has become a mirror: a place of waiting, of questioning, of unfinished reconciliation. And that, too, is a form of pilgrimage.

I turned the page of my first Camino diary and read words that now feel almost prophetic—written in the shadow of a troubled mind, at a time when I believed so much of life still depended on me. *"We live in a world of human beings, animals, and plants, all subject to the forces of nature and events. Some bring joy, some sadness, and others suffering and hardship. Nothing in the natural world is free of pain in some form. We tend to shy away from difficulty, ruin, and sorrow, preferring the soft option, yet no growth comes without pain. If we accept that pain can teach us, that it can strengthen us, then in the long run we may live this life— whatever comes upon us—making the most of that one long day called life, before we leave this mortal coil.*

I am not advocating that we seek darkness rather than light. But if darkness comes, let us embrace it and get on with living as best we can, right now. This pilgrimage of the Camino has been a journey—a long walk from one place to another, in body and in mind, with a spirit of adventure I did not expect. It has been, and will continue to be, a holy work long after I reach Santiago. A chance to encounter mystery—not just to breathe."

Reading those words now, I felt both closeness and distance. They had once carried my deepest longings, absorbed into my heart with conviction and hope. Yet I could also see how much remained unresolved. Understanding pain will complete the work. Now I know that insight alone does not finish the journey. I have come to realise that I still have a long way to go on this inward path—perhaps farther than any outward Camino I might yet walk. I still feel the pull of the road, the desire to repeat the journey in body once more. But I ask myself now, with gentler honesty: *to what avail?*

The walking never truly ends. The question is whether I am willing to keep walking inward, where no yellow arrows mark the way.

Through all my adventures and wanderings, The Way has remained a quiet presence, returning in moments of stillness and movement alike, gently reminding me of paths once walked and of an inner journey that continues to unfold.

Chapter 11. To Leon, in my mind.

It was Sunday morning, and once again I woke late. I took it as a sign that I had settled emotionally to a greater degree after so much tramping of The Way. Until then, I had been unaccustomed to sleeping more than a few hours at a time. For the first four hundred kilometres or so, my emotions had run high—restless, raw, and often unresolved. Now it seemed I had crossed a threshold, at least in body and mind, if not yet entirely in spirit.

My stomach no longer grumbled after my familiar breakfast ritual, and before long, I was back on The Way. Having walked out of historic Burgos—reworking the landscape of El Cid in my imagination and absorbing the Gothic grandeur of that great city—the villages and towns ahead became milestones rather than destinations.

Castrojeriz, Frómista, and Carrión de los Condes marked my gradual introduction to the Meseta's wasteland. It's wide-open spaces, the sounds of unseen wildlife, and the endless crop fields waiting for the first drop of rain at this time of year, but now drought shapes the plains and my days. When I was not walking alongside other pilgrims, nature itself became my companion—the land, the silence, the sky, and the small oasis villages scattered like punctuation marks across the emptiness.

Those medieval towns—**Sahagún and El Burgo Ranero**—were like paintings half-asleep in the sun. Quiet villages and modest hamlets offered brief refuge and gentle distraction from the monotony of the Meseta before the terrain once again rose and tested me. Each shift in landscape demanded something different: patience, endurance, surrender. And so I walked on, carried by the rhythm of my steps, learning—slowly—that the Camino teaches not only through effort and hardship, but also through stillness, repetition, and the long spaces in between.

The final nineteen kilometres into **León** were as painful as my entry into Burgos had been—save for one thing. That time, I had been accompanied from a distance by two Spanish beauties, their presence easing the weight of the road. This time, there was no such grace. The Way to me then was a lonely, tiring, tortured march.

With every step, it felt as though hot pokers were being driven into my toes. I kept going anyway, trudging forward toward the goal I had once imagined would carry meaning—León. I had expected some symbolic reward at the end of this long stretch, a *Sword of Discernment* perhaps, something to mark the passage. Instead, there was only pain. No symbolism. Just endurance.

A passing pilgrim offered me his last anti-inflammatories. I swallowed them without ceremony, and by the time I reached the outskirts of León, they had begun to take effect. Within the hour, the sharpest edge of pain eased, just enough to keep me moving.

Earlier that day, I had strolled along quaint paved roads and ancient Roman stone paths into **Mansilla de las Mulas,** admiring the remains of a once-fortified town rebuilt in the thirteenth and fourteenth centuries. Its walls were again crumbling, yet two original gates and a tower staircase remained nearly perfect, as if time had deliberately spared them. León now loomed closer. The final seven kilometres took me through industrial outskirts — harsh, functional, and uninviting. Bridges and overpasses made the Way safer despite heavy traffic, and the yellow arrows faithfully guided me through detours. I stopped just short of the town to eat the last of my supplies: dry bread, a tin of sardines, and a small piece of cheese.

The outskirts of León were run down. Slum dwellings pressed in close. Old posters of long-gone matadors peeled from dirty walls. Graffiti scarred shuttered shops and broken windows. Ragged figures lingered in the shade of alleyways, waiting for the sun to drop below the skyline—or perhaps waiting for the next fix before slipping back into the shadows behind their eyes.

I considered buying water from one of the rundown shops, but thought better of it. Thirst was preferable to regret. And so I followed the rough, hand-painted yellow arrows onward, toward the heart of the city. Toward whatever waited there.

As I moved closer to the city centre, my spirits lifted, and the surroundings softened. The harshness of the outskirts gave way to beauty, order, and the quiet dignity of age. The first resident I encountered was a middle-aged Spanish woman who approached me and offered me a place to stay for the night. I could not tell whether she meant a bed in her home or something more personal. Either way, I declined politely. My mind was fixed elsewhere—on the heart of my journey and the faint, persistent image of a *Sword of Discernment* that had begun to form in my imagination. It was less an object now than a symbol, hovering somewhere between hope and exhaustion.

León itself seemed to rise around me as a witness to history. Established as a permanent settlement by the Roman military as early as 29 BC, the city once served as a staging point for Galician gold on its way to Rome. That ancient purpose—guardianship, vigilance, protection—felt strangely relevant to my own inner search.

I was stunned by León's beauty. Even through the pain of blistered feet and the dull ache of fatigue, the city spoke to me. My spiritual longing and physical suffering walked side by side now, neither cancelling the other. And so I continued inward, carried by both—the quest still alive, the body still protesting, the city unfolding around me like an answer not yet spoken, and by the time I found the pilgrim hostel, night had already begun to settle over León. The city's earlier brilliance faded into softer outlines—stone walls glowing faintly under streetlights, footsteps echoing where voices had been. Inside the hostel, the rituals were familiar and wordless: boots off, pack down, bed claimed. No explanations were needed. Everyone there carried the same tired look, the same inward turning.

The silence was not absolute, but it was respected. A rustle of sleeping bags. The clink of a water bottle. Someone breathing deeply, already gone. I tended to my feet with practised care, draining blisters, applying ointment, wrapping them gently as though they belonged to someone else. Pain had become a companion by then—not dramatic, just present. Lying there in the dark, the day replayed itself without invitation. The long approach. The loss of expectation. The imagined sword had dissolved into nothing more than endurance. I realised then that nothing had been taken from me—only illusions. And that, too, was a form of reckoning.

There was no voice, no revelation, no sudden clarity. Just a quiet knowing that the Camino was stripping me back, not granting me symbols but asking me to live without them. Whatever discernment I was seeking would not be handed to me at the gates of a city. It would have to be carried, earned, and recognised long after the walking stopped.

Sleep came slowly, but it came—and with it, a fragile peace—enough for one night.

As I wandered the ancient streets in search of a café for an early breakfast, a thought arose unbidden: *Could this be the City of God?* Was this the place of fiery spirituality that would finally bring me to peace?

Perhaps I had listened too closely to other pilgrims along the way, their voices glowing with reverence for León. Maybe I had absorbed too much of their certainty, borrowed too freely from their beliefs and interpretations. Or perhaps this longing was simply a residue of childhood—an old inheritance of faith, half-remembered and never thoroughly examined.

These seemingly impossible dreams and aspirations may have served only as motivation, a way of keeping myself moving forward on the road. Like **Don Quixote,** I was chasing windmills while convincing myself they were giants. It would not have been the first time. And as that thought settled, so too did the realisation that letting go of the dream did not mean failure—it might, in fact, be the beginning of something more honest.

I put the diary down for a moment and sat with the thought. Yes, I had learned to surrender much—partly through my Camino experiences, and partly through the deeper understanding that sometimes you have to surrender everything to gain anything of real value. I reassured myself that not having an answer yet did not mean the end of my search for inner clarity or spiritual wellness. It simply meant the journey was unfinished.

I took my time wandering through the city, exploring the monuments of the past, feeling the vibration of ancient relics worn smooth by centuries of devotion. And then, not far away,

I found myself absorbed into the pace of a modern metropolis —traffic, noise, urgency.

The contrast was stark, yet seamless. Old and new, sacred and ordinary, exist side by side. It was like looking into a mirror and seeing the past and present merge into one reflection, neither diminishing the other.

It was there that I found my way into the square that holds León's finest treasure—the sublime Gothic cathedral. Its magnificent stained-glass windows streamed light into the vast interior, illuminating the sacred with colour and grace. The serene statue of the *Virgen Blanca* welcomed me from her place below the central tympanum, her presence both gentle and commanding. The choir stalls, intricately carved with biblical figures alongside creative and humorous depictions of human vice, reminded me of the cheek and genius of Michelangelo's Sistine Chapel ceiling murals in Florence. Within the seven chapels of the cathedral lie Gothic tombs, including that of King Ordoño II, King of Galicia from 910 and later King of León from 914—a pivotal figure in the reconquest of the Iberian Peninsula and a military leader against the Moors. Enshrined near his tomb was a powerful scene of the Crucifixion, grounding the space in sacrifice and devotion.

At the heart of the cathedral rested the legacy of Rodrigo Díaz de Vivar—the medieval Spanish military leader known to all as *El Cid*, "the Master." His presence seemed to echo through the stone, a reminder of a time when faith, power, and identity were inseparable.

The experience drew me far from modern-day León. Eventually, I retraced my steps to a nearby café, sitting outside with a coffee and a light Spanish lunch, content to watch the steady parade of pilgrims pass by—some familiar faces who stopped to chat, others strangers continuing their own journeys. For the first time in a long while, I felt a profound sense of freedom, unburdened by the usual responsibilities of life.

I finished the afternoon by strolling across the plaza from the basilica and taking a long walk around the city's outskirts, absorbing yet more of its beauty. There and then, I made a quiet vow to myself: I would return to this great city one day. I would spend more time exploring its sacred art museums, its Romanesque sculptures, and I would return once more to the cathedral—to be bathed again in the light of those stained-glass windows, and perhaps even to attend Mass there on a Sunday.

The second night at the Albergue León Benedictina was a fitting end to my stay in the city of my dreams on the Camino. Although I had observed the local tradition of a summer afternoon siesta—sleeping for about an hour to escape the heat—I was still weary from the road. Around six o'clock, I returned to the street and headed to a nearby bar for a cool drink. It was there that I met Sandy, a retired Canadian airline employee. Sandy had walked the Camino the previous summer and had since returned to give back to the Way by volunteering at the very albergue where I was staying. He worked long ten-hour days, allocating beds, issuing clean linen to arriving pilgrims, and keeping a watchful, caring eye on everyone—much like a dormitory master in a boarding school.

There was no fanfare in what he did, no sermon or explanation—just presence. In that simplicity, I sensed something I had been searching for: a faith no longer driven by striving or expectation, but by service freely given. It struck me that perhaps this, too, was part of the Camino's teaching—that the journey does not always end at a cathedral door or in a moment of revelation, but sometimes in the unnoticed acts that make the road easier for others.

This kind of generosity toward the Camino was something I had noticed before, even on my first pilgrimage. There was a quiet tradition among some pilgrims of returning—not to walk again, but to serve. To my pleasant surprise, I would meet Sandy once more in Santiago at the end of the Way, where he was working in the office where I collected my Camino certificate, selling rosary beads of all things.

That night, I returned to bed early—my first truly restful early night on the Camino. In the silence of the dormitory, surrounded by the soft breathing of fellow pilgrims, I sensed that something within me had loosened its grip. Not answers, but a willingness to continue without them. And for the first time in days, that was enough.

Morning came gently in León. There was no urgency in it, no call to arms or trumpet of revelation. I rose quietly from my bunk, careful not to disturb the others, and packed my few belongings with the practised movements of a pilgrim who had learned that nothing truly belongs to him on the road. Outside, the city was stirring—cafés setting out chairs, delivery trucks idling, early commuters moving with purpose. León was returning to itself, and I, once again, to the Way.

As I stepped beyond the albergue's shelter and followed the familiar yellow arrows toward the city's outskirts, I felt the subtle shift that always accompanied departure. The sacred gave way to the ordinary. Stone cathedrals faded into footpaths and roads, incense into the smell of diesel and morning bread. My feet, still tender from León's long entry, reminded me that whatever had been gained inwardly would have to be carried outward—step by step, blister by blister.

In my earlier years, I would have left a city like León, sure of what it meant. I would have wrapped the experience in neat conclusions—this place had changed me, that moment had answered my questions, this symbol had confirmed my beliefs. Faith, then, was something solid and declarative, a structure as firm as the cathedral walls I had admired the day before. But now, I walked on with far less certainty—and, strangely, with more peace.

The older pilgrim I had become no longer demanded answers from the road or from God. León had not delivered the revelation I once imagined would come with such a place. Yet, it had given me something truer: the recognition that ambiguity is not the enemy of faith, but often its companion. The Camino was teaching me—again—that clarity does not always arrive when summoned, and meaning cannot be forced into existence by longing alone.

This tension would arise again not far down the track. I did not yet know where or how, only that the pattern was familiar. Each stage of the Camino seemed to invite hope, strip it bare, and then offer something quieter in its place. Youth seeks certainty so it can stand firm. Maturity learns to walk without it.

As León receded behind me, I understood that the actual work of the Camino was not in collecting spiritual highs or sacred experiences, but in learning how to let go of expectations, of outcomes, of the need to be right or resolved. What remained was movement, breath, and trust in the unfolding path.

And so I walked on—uncertain, unarmoured, and quietly receptive—back into the physical world of dust, road, and rhythm, carrying with me the unspoken understanding that the Camino does not end in a city, nor in a moment of insight, but in the continual act of surrendering to the next step.

Chapter 12. Beyond the New Horizon.

As I tramped away from León, the city unfolded behind me as a mirror image recalled in motion—its meandering milestones slipping past in quiet succession: museums, parks, gardens, overpass bridges, and flowing streams that softened the city's edge. I paused at one of the last cafés on the Way, seated at an outdoor table overlooking a broad sweep of parkland, and allowed myself a final reckoning with the place I was leaving. Later, I would struggle to describe León adequately, but in that moment, an image formed that stayed with me. It felt to me like the *Champ de Mars* in Paris—minus the Eiffel Tower and the shimmer of the Seine. Instead, the Bernesga River flowed directly through León, soon joined by the Torío, which in turn fed into the Esla, a tributary of the great Douro. This intricate river system, stretching throughout the province of León and including the Sil with its dramatic canyons at El Bierzo, spoke of a land shaped quietly and persistently by water. It was all part of León's rich hydrography—life-giving, understated, and enduring.

The landscape of León itself reminded me of something far more domestic and familiar: a plain white tablecloth from my childhood. Clean, unadorned, without fancy crocheted frills along the edge. I pictured it clearly—the cloth without ornamentation, without excess. To me, León was Paris all over again, but stripped back. Paris without the frills.
I ordered a second breakfast—my last indulgence before the road carried me fully onward—and settled for coffee and a croissant, a habit that would continue whenever opportunity allowed in the days ahead. It was there, lingering longer than necessary, that I met Dan from Prague. He would prove to be fine company on the next leg of the journey toward Santiago. Once again, the Camino reminded me that just as places leave

their imprint, so too do people—often arriving quietly, precisely when they are needed.

So Dan and I set out together toward **Chozas de Abajo,** and, at his suggestion, we agreed on a shared goal for the day: the *Refugio de Jesús*, some 21 kilometres south. Dan had stayed there the previous summer when he completed the same leg of the Camino from León, and he spoke of it with a familiarity that carried confidence. I was content to follow.

We broke off for lunch in a small village just off the beaten path. Dan drank only tonic water. He had long ago settled into the habit of eating just one meal a day, a practice that reached back to his childhood. His family, he explained, could afford little more. Over time, he had learned that the bubbles in the tonic seemed to give him energy, and from that moment on, I nicknamed him *Bubbles*—a name that suited both his drink and his quietly buoyant spirit.

Dan's father had been an academic, with a particular passion for teaching his children the history of the Czech Republic. Money was scarce, and train fares for educational excursions were beyond reach. The compromise was stark but purposeful: one meal a day in exchange for knowledge. Hunger, in that household, became the price paid for a deeper inheritance—an education rooted in story, place, and memory. As Dan told it, there was no bitterness in his voice, only acceptance.

We arrived later at **Villar de Mazarife** and paid our dues for the night at the Refugio de Jesús. It was a fascinating place— set slightly off the main route—, and at first glance it resembled a kind of pilgrim's ark. The walls, from floor to ceiling, were covered with drawings, prayers, names, confessions, and fragments of thought, scrawled by pilgrims over many decades. It was as though the building itself had absorbed the voices of those who had passed through it.

Among the youthful comments and sketches, one quote stood out. Written boldly on the wall was a passage from Jack Kerouac's *On the Road*:

"They danced down the streets like dingledodies, and I shambled after, as I've been doing all my life, after people who interest me, because the only people who interest me are the mad ones, the ones mad to live, mad to talk, mad to be saved, desirous of everything at the same time, the ones that never yawn or say a commonplace thing, but burn, burn, burn like fabulous yellow Roman candles exploding like spiders across the stars…"

Kerouac's word *dingledodies*—his affectionate name for the beautiful misfits he was forever drawn to—felt perfectly placed here. Looking around that ark-like refuge, filled with the traces of countless wanderers, I knew exactly what he meant. And I knew, too, that on this Camino, I was still shambling after them—those mad enough to walk, to question, to burn brightly for a while, and then move on.

Like every other room in the place, ours was covered in graffiti from floor to ceiling, yet despite the layers of ink and memory, it was reasonably clean. I took a hot shower, changed into fresh clothes, and hung my washing out to dry before joining Dan in the courtyard for a drink—mine a zero-alcohol beer, his another bottle of sparkling water.

As night closed in, I found myself sitting with a free-thinking English girl. We talked easily about the stages of our Camino journeys, the minor mishaps of the day, and the laughter that came from meeting fellow pilgrims along The Way. She was a schoolteacher, and I confessed—half joking—that I had already had my fair share of failed relationships with teachers. She laughed, firmly in the spirit of her profession, and suggested that perhaps I should consider a different occupation if I ever found myself drawn into another relationship. I smiled and quietly filed that advice away for some future date.

Only later did I come to realise that it mattered little what a woman's occupation was. The pattern was always the same. Whenever I turned toward the heart of a woman in preference to the deeper call of God within, I seemed to invite the same old heartache. It was a lesson still forming then—one that would return, further down the road, asking not to be resisted but gently surrendered to.

We walked the same road, yet we were not walking the same Camino. For the young men beside me, each step was an act of becoming. Their packs were light not only with youth, but with expectation. The road ahead shimmered with possibility—careers yet to be chosen, loves yet to be tested, beliefs still firm enough to lean upon without question. They spoke of what they would do, who they would be, and where life might take them once Santiago lay behind them. Hope moved them forward like a strong, steady wind at their backs.

For me, the road asked something different.

I was not walking toward a future so much as walking away from what had already broken. Where memories carried ambition, I carried accumulation—loss layered upon loss, faith worn thin at the edges, dreams once held tightly now loosened by time and disappointment. Their pilgrimage was a reaching; mine was a yielding. Each step I took was less about arrival and more about release.

At rest stops, they planned. I reflected. At dawn, they surged ahead. I paced myself. They sought confirmation; I sought quiet. And yet the Camino made no distinction. It offered the same dust, the same blistering heat, the same rising hills to us all. Hope and surrender shared the same footprints. Youth and weariness drank from the same fountains. The road did not ask *why* we walked—only that we did.

Somewhere between **Hospital de Órbigo** and the climb toward **Mount Irago,** I began to understand that surrender was not the opposite of hope, but its deeper cousin. Hope says, *something awaits me ahead.* Surrender whispers, *what I need may already be within me.*

Their pilgrimage leaned forward into becoming. Mine leaned inward into acceptance. Both were holy in their own way. And perhaps that is the Camino's quiet truth: that no matter our age, we are always walking two roads at once—the one beneath our feet, and the one unfolding unseen within.

Only now, rereading those pages, did I recall how I had fallen behind the young men. One by one, they had pulled ahead, their longer strides and unbroken momentum carrying them onward, while my pace softened under heat and reflection. Roland, the elder among them, had fallen back too, and I slowed instinctively, hoping he might catch up so that at least one familiar presence would remain beside me. But that was not to be.

Roland, wiser perhaps than the rest of us, chose another way. When the heat grew cruel and the road unforgiving, he boarded a train and travelled on to Santiago ahead of us all. There was no shame in his decision—only discernment. At the time, I barely noticed; now I recognise it as another quiet lesson from the road: knowing when to walk on, and when to let go.

We were all heading toward the mountain village of **Foncebadón**, a place wrapped in legend and warning—the town of savage dogs, or so the stories went. One of the keenest of the young pilgrim brothers had spoken earnestly of the limited accommodation there. He and Dan had stayed the previous year and urged me, almost pleading, to make the effort. I had promised him in a phone message that I would try, and if he saved me a bed, I joked, I would kiss the foot of his bandaged leg in gratitude.

Before the climb, I caught up briefly with two Italians I had walked with the day before—Marcus, a cotton textile manufacturer, and his striking partner, Marfuaus, a fashion consultant. Marcus spoke no English, so Marfuaus became our interpreter, moving gracefully between languages as easily as she did between worlds. The three of us sat together at a small café in Rabanal del Camino, sharing snacks and drinks and talking about business, creativity, and the strange freedom of being momentarily unmoored from ordinary life. As dusk settled, I bid them farewell, knowing our paths were about to diverge.

Many pilgrims chose to stay the night there, resting before the steep ascent into the mountains. I considered it too. Yet something restless stirred within me, and as evening deepened, I chose instead to begin the climb toward **Foncebadón**. Leaving **Rabanal del Camino,** the village perched just above the valley floor on the mountain pass, had long been a place of refuge. **The Knights Templar** had established a fort there in medieval times, offering protection to pilgrims from wolves, bandits, and the lawless dangers of the high country. It was said the village bore traces of both Christian and Muslim influence, and legend held that one of Charlemagne's knights had married a Muslim woman there— a quiet reminder that even in an age of division, lives and faiths once intertwined.

As I climbed into the falling light, alone now, the Camino narrowed again—not just in geography, but in meaning. Youth had surged ahead. Companions had peeled away. Comfort lay behind me. What remained was the mountain, the darkening path, and the unspoken invitation to trust whatever lay beyond the next bend.

And so I walked on—upward, slower, and quieter—carrying less certainty than before, but perhaps more willingness to surrender to whatever the night and the road were preparing to teach me next.

As I climbed into the falling light, alone now, the Camino narrowed again—not just in geography, but in meaning. Youth had surged ahead. Companions had peeled away. Comfort lay behind me. What remained was the mountain, the darkening path, and the unspoken invitation to trust whatever lay beyond the next bend. And so I walked on—upward, slower, and quieter—carrying less certainty than before, but perhaps more willingness to surrender to whatever the night and the road were preparing to teach me next.

I recalled the steep ascent toward my destination for the night stretched 4.5 kilometres to the crest, where Foncebadón sat scattered among weathered stone buildings, a few donkeys, and—so it seemed—more wild dogs than passing pilgrims. The heat still pressed heavily upon me as I reached a point halfway up the mountain, and it was there I realised I had run out of water. My mouth was dry, my throat tight, and the weight of the climb suddenly felt more real.

Then, as if placed there by providence, I rounded a bend in the cliff face and found a simple water trough, a tap meant for livestock, fed by a nearby spring. I drank deeply, refilled my flasks, and then sat down to soak my feet in the icy stream. The cold bit sharply, then soothed, and I rested there longer than I had intended.

For a moment, I considered camping there for the night, beneath the open sky. I felt free—calm in body, clear in mind, and strangely relaxed in spirit. There was no fear in the thought of sleeping alone in such an isolated place, no anxiety about wild dogs or the darkness gathering around me. It felt, briefly, like a perfect stillness.

Yet after a time, wisdom—or perhaps belonging—nudged me onward. I rose, dried my feet, laced up my boots and shouldered my pack once more. I decided to continue to Foncebadón and seek out the Monte Irago albergue, hoping the young rock-star musician among my band of brothers had indeed saved me a bed.

With the sun sinking and the mountain quiet around me, I climbed on, leaving behind the temptation of solitude for the possibility of shared shelter, carrying with me the calm reassurance that on this road, what one needs often appears just in time.

Foncebadón was another of those moments that felt less like real life and more like a movie set—much like **Ávila** had a few days earlier. It looked as though Clint Eastwood might step out from behind a crumbling stone wall at any moment, squinting into the sun of some late-1960s spaghetti western. The old Roman road cut straight through the village, once a vital route in imperial times. After the Romans withdrew, it faded into obscurity, only to become a hermitage for monks in the tenth century. For centuries, it lay almost abandoned, until the late 1980s, when its crumbling stone cottages, rusted gates, and sagging roofs were reborn as a refuge for modern pilgrims after the Camino was rerouted.

Reading back through my diary now, I noted that I arrived at the Monte Irago albergue late in the evening to find an astonishing number of pilgrims gathered around an enormous paella being cooked in a pan big enough to bathe in.

The air was thick with hunger and garlic. I could make out rice—perhaps risotto—capsicum, onions, whole cloves of garlic, squid, peas, and maybe parsley. I was desperate for a bed, and now equally desperate for a plate of whatever holy concoction was bubbling away.

The kitchen doubled as reception, and the young Spaniard cooking the paella—long-haired, greasy, and looking as though he hadn't slept indoors for years—paid me absolutely no attention. So I waited. And waited. While doing so, I studied the old photographs on the wall, including one that struck me deeply: an Indian sage in flowing robes, gripping a walking staff crowned with a large crucifix. The image was faded, hanging crookedly on a grimy wall, but it radiated something ancient and sincere. I remember thinking that the young Spaniards running the place were perhaps his latter-day disciples—ragged, barefoot, and unconcerned with worldly order.

Eventually, another long-haired youth appeared, equally unkempt, dressed in a dirt-stained robe and holding a mangy-looking cat tucked under his arm. In broken English, he asked what I wanted.

"A bed," I said, simply. The young Spaniard waved me away without ceremony. "No bed left."

I tried again. "I'm Doug—from Australia. Robin, the young German pilgrim, said he would reserve one for me."

His eyes widened. "Aww! Señor Australia—you have a bed."

Just like that. Grace arrives when it chooses.

I made my way to the back of the albergue, weaving past sheep, goats, chickens, and a mule, and there I found Robin heading toward an outdoor basin to wash his clothes. True to my word—and without a shred of dignity left in me—I dropped to one knee and kissed his bare, tattooed leg. I was simply that grateful.

And so, at the edge of the mountain, in a village reborn from ruins, among strangers, animals, and saints in disguise, I was given shelter for the night. On the Camino, I was learning again and again that surrender often comes disguised as absurdity—and grace rarely announces itself politely.

Chapter 13. A New Pathway.

I sat there in a vacant, pensive mood, recalling my stay at the Monte Irago albergue—sleeping above an animal shelter, lying out on a thin mat beside the Italian couple who had decided, after all, to climb the mountain in the evening. I smiled to myself, remembering our parting exchange. Marcus had said something to me in Italian on our parenting farewell the next morning. Curious, I asked Marfuaus, his beautiful partner, what he had said. She smiled and replied, "He says he will never forget your smiling face—and he will always remember your snoring." I laughed quietly at that.

Another memory surfaced: earlier that evening, I had been stretching at the front of the room, showing a pilgrim a few simple yoga exercises to ease cramped muscles. I turned around mid-stretch to find the entire albergue—every mat-dweller in the place—following along in solemn unison, as if I had accidentally become the abbot of some barefoot order of the flexible and exhausted. That strange *knowing*—of what needs to be done when nothing else will do—had not escaped me then, nor has it now, even in my dotage.

And that was not all. The change that was to follow in me was already in motion. I recalled the poem I had written after my fall in Paris, one I shared with the young German rock musician during the midnight hours while he played his guitar. A month late, he emailed me, asking for a copy of the lyrics. What followed surprised me even then: two of my poems were later set to music on his upcoming albums.

This Camino had been cathartic. I had fallen into the well of darkness—depression, despair, and fear—terrified of the dragon I believed waited at the bottom. Yet what I encountered there was not a dragon's mouth, but a lotus flower: a blooming of creative ideas. Even now, years later, I am still living that dream—writing books, writing songs, watching the outflow continue.

And yet, in the quiet recesses of my mind, I could still hear a voice whispering, *"Be careful of residual parachutes."*
Were the writings and the songs simply a way of slowing my fall toward the sacred? Or was I still afraid to let go completely?

I believed then—and still do—that the God of my own understanding had led me to that place. What came next, however, was up to me. Perhaps this return to my old Camino diaries was precisely what I needed: to acknowledge where I had been, to take honest stock of what I had done, and to move forward again, trusting that God would continue to lead the way. And then there was that other voice from long ago, steady and patient, returning once more: *"Trust in the slow work of God."*

My mind drifted then to the **Cruz de Ferro,** one of the highest points on the entire Camino Francés. A tall wooden pole crowned with an iron cross, it stands stark against the sky. Long before it became Christian, it was an ancient Celtic monument, later adopted by the Romans and dedicated to Mercury, the god and protector of travellers. In the ninth century, a hermit named Gaucelmo crowned it with a cross, and it was absorbed into the Christian imagination as a place of surrender.

For centuries, pilgrims have carried their burdens to this place —symbolised by a stone, a token, or some small object of personal meaning—to be laid down and left behind. Over time, the offerings have formed a mound at the base of the cross, a quiet hill of accumulated grief, regret, hope, repentance, and release—a graveyard of yesterday's pain.
There is something eerie about the place. The air feels charged, as if memory itself lingers there. Some pilgrims cry openly. Others sing softly, songs of letting go. Many stand in silence, choked by the moment, suspended between past and future, simply surrendering to the now.

When my turn came, I placed a small wooden token at the base of the cross—an emblem of the Templar knights. It felt fitting then: the warrior laying down his sword, or at least the illusion of it. I did not know it would not be my last visit to this place.

Within four years, I would stand there again, this time carrying a different burden. I would set down a pair of glasses, pressed into the stones, in memory of my son Peter, who had passed by his own hand. The Cruz de Ferro would no longer be symbolic alone—it would be personal, irreversible, and sacred in a way I could not yet imagine. For any pilgrim, life will ask us to return—deeper, emptier, more human—to surrender again. And still, the cross stands. The stones remain. A nd the road goes on.

Perhaps that is the truth of the Camino: we lay something down, believing we are finished with it, only to discover that in my reflections on that time now passed, I am mindful of the quiet beauty found in the lessons of suffering. They return to me as cherished moments, symbolic now perhaps, yet no less true. On that first journey, I was given back the voice of my early childhood, and through it, the deeper contours of my passage into adulthood. The young pilgrim I was then—and the one I remain now—walked the Way as a rite of passage.

Mine did not come easily, nor in the customary ways. It came through abandonment, fragile health, misadventure, and the hard-won pain of letting go of all I thought I was. That Camino marked the beginning of my gathering of wisdom. In the years that followed, I learned to give voice to my inner life through stories and songs—finding direction not in certainty but in expression.

And yet, as I sit here now recalling that journey, I see another layer revealed. In returning to those memories, I am reliving a rite of passage once more—the surrender of those who chose to abandon me: family, friends, acquaintances, even foes, alike in their judgment and disdain. Yes, I have come a long way; that much is true.

I walked the Camino to let go, to seek love, and at times I found only its pale reflection—lust mistaken for belonging. So I returned again and again, until the lesson no longer needed to be learned. Now, if I were to return once more, it would not be for taking, but for giving back—not from the darkness, nor even from the light, but from a place of simple presence. Perhaps this is the learning of my later years: how to live fully in the day that is given.

And so I return to these old diary entries, to the books I have written chof the Camino—not to relive the past, but to recall and refresh the heart for the here and now. I do this for you, the reader, and for the continuing work of my own soul.

My young band of brothers lay ahead of me. Dan, true to his custom, had left before dawn. Robin, Young, and I had walked close together at first, talking softly about our pilgrimage and the day before—about our personal acts of letting go at the foot of the Cruz de Ferro.

Soon our words thinned, and we walked in silence down the steady slope toward the small *Refugio de Manjarín*, hosted by Tomás, who considered himself the last of the Templar knights and offered drinks and simple sustenance to passing pilgrims. His rustic outpost was even more primitive than our previous night's shelter—no running water, no electricity—yet it became another indelible memory of the Way.

A rough, hand-written sign hung from the verandah of this knightly abode, marking distances to Santiago and other cities along the Camino, as if time itself had been pinned there with charcoal and faith. From **Manjarín,** we walked on through fields of heather, arriving at a large cairn that opened onto a breathtaking view of **Ponferrada**, far below on the valley floor.

From there, we began the sharp descent—nearly four kilometres down to **El Acebo**. Once again, the seriousness we sometimes carried fell away, replaced by the quiet companionship of shared pace and inward attention. Gradually, we opened to one another again, trading stories and jokes to distract ourselves from the midsummer sun beating down upon us.

We had taken it upon ourselves to leave minor motivational signs for Roland, wherever he might be treading his own path. Robin had received a message that Roland was six hours behind us. What we did not know then was that Roland, in his own wisdom, had caught a train to Santiago and was enjoying rest, good food, wine, and release from the rigours of the pilgrim's way.

Before long, I fell behind Robin and Young. I assumed I would catch them by nightfall. Dan, I knew, was already far ahead and would likely keep it that way—he preferred his rite of passage to be a solitary experience, walking the Way alone, listening only to his own footsteps and the silence that followed them.

It was then that I began to realise I was meant to be the adult —the mature one—yet this young band of brothers had helped me touch parts of my youth I had long overlooked. They stirred memories and sensibilities I had buried beneath the weight of responsibility and survival. I came to see that it would take more than this Camino alone to release my own rite of passage fully and to step, with honesty, into the reality of a mature adulthood—one shaped not by proving, but by service.

Even then, I sensed that my return to the Camino in years to come might not be for learning alone, but for giving: to walk in service to fellow pilgrims, in thought, word, and deed. Who knows? The Camino has its own way of teaching its lessons, often revealing them only when we believe we have already learned enough. I would come to understand this more fully on my second and third Caminos, but for now, I was still gathering the first fruits of insight in the company of my small band of brothers.

They spoke freely of the emotional neglect and unhealthy patterns they had endured at the hands of parents, and of the survival skills those experiences had forced upon them. I listened, aware that here I was—an older man—still cautious, still measured, still reluctant to speak openly of wounds that belonged to a distant past. In this way, they were far ahead of me in letting go, yet far behind in the kind of wisdom that only lived experience grants. Their vision was still turned toward the future unfolding before them. Mine was bent toward the long work of release—of loosening the grip of what had already been lived. They were dreaming forward; I was learning, still, how to lay the past down gently and walk on unburdened.

The diary entry carried me back into that final hundred kilometres—from **Ponferrada to Sarria**—stirring memories of fear and pain I had not yet learned how to face. They were buried then, set aside for another day. Like an old soldier, whose memories of love are not merely the legacy of words, books, or songs, but something forged and carried within, this Camino awakened an inner figure—part Templar knight, part Viking standing before his final funeral fire.

From the imposing Templar castle of Ponferrada, slowly fading behind me, the Way softened into the lush pastures of El Bierzo, cradled by mountains. I remembered the flavours of exquisitely cured meats, the sweetness of ripe cherries offered by village hands, and the quiet grace of the gardens at the Iglesia de Santiago in Villafranca del Bierzo. Passing through the Puerto de Perdón—the Gate of Forgiveness—felt then, as it does now, like nourishment for the heart rather than the body, a spiritual sustenance I did not yet know how to name.

The Way followed the murmuring river Valcarce before demanding the long ascent into the **O Cebreiro range** and the **Sierra do Courel**. We crossed the rugged contours of the Ancares Mountains and descended from the **Alto do Poio** into **Triacastela,** where the land seemed to breathe history into every step. The **San Xil** route unfolded with a beauty that fortified my pilgrim spirit, while a narrow forest path—taken with Young—slipped quietly through ancient Galician oak woods. We chose the alternate way through Samos, walking in the shadow of its monastery, where monks had preserved centuries of prayer, scholarship, and the earliest threads of Spanish history.

It was there, in **Galicia**, that we first tasted freshly cooked octopus—simple, communal, unforgettable. It was also where the darker edge of Celtic memory revealed itself: symbolic witches staring from windows of houses and albergues, existing alongside the unmistakable presence of Christian imagery. Light and shadow lived together here without apology, each reminding the pilgrim of forces older than doctrine.

And as we entered **Sarria,** we were reminded—quietly but unmistakably—that only one hundred kilometres remained. From here, every step would count toward Santiago, toward the Compostela, the simple certificate that proved we had walked the final stretch. Yet even then, I sensed that no parchment could ever certify what had truly been walked, endured, remembered, or surrendered along the Way.

I was recalling now the previous seven hundred kilometres and the people I had met along our shared pilgrimages. Faces rose and fell in my mind like stations of memory, each carrying a fragment of the Way. I thought of the young German backpacker I had met in the Pyrenees on that very first day, when we had both run out of water. The mountain had offered no mercy then—only heat, exposure, and the humbling realisation of our limits. Strangers until that moment, we were bound by necessity, by thirst, and by the unspoken understanding that the Camino would strip us bare long before it carried us forward.

We shared what little we had, laughed at our miscalculation, and moved on together for a time—two pilgrims learning early that survival on the Way was never meant to be a solitary act. That encounter, fleeting as it was, became a quiet initiation: a lesson in trust, in vulnerability, and in the grace that arrives when pride finally loosens its grip.

Looking back now, I see how the Camino introduced itself to me through that simple act of running out of water. It was not a punishment, but a warning and a promise all at once—*you will be emptied, and you will be sustained*. In that exchange on the Pyrenean ridge, the long journey ahead revealed its first truth: nothing of value is carried alone, and nothing essential is ever truly lost when it is shared.

Like meeting the Irish mother and daughter, who carried with them the stories of the land of my ancestors, their words awakened something long dormant in me. The open spirits of the two Canadian schoolteachers were generous with humour and curiosity. The Danish artist and his actor son, walking side by side between generations, teach me how creativity passes quietly from one soul to another.

There was laughter and song with the Dutch kids, carefree and alive in the moment; singing with the Belgians; listening in stillness to the beautiful voices of the South Africans as they lifted hymns and harmonies into the open air. And my young German rock-star friend, whose presence would have a profound influence—drawing me inward toward my own creative self, becoming a cathartic means of survival when words alone were not enough. Other shades of the past drifted by: the Greeks and the Italians, spirited and expressive; time shared with the French; the quiet magnetism of Spanish beauties, both seen and unseen. The influence of the English schoolteacher lingered as a lesson in freedom, while the fierce determination of the retired German ballet teacher revealed discipline born of devotion and pain. She had handed me her business card with a German mantra embossed with the words translation into English " Oh Lord! I learnt to dance so that angels in heaven knew that they should not mess with me."

Above all, I remember the kindness—genuine, unguarded kindness—of pilgrim souls along the Way: the volunteers in albergues, the generosity of strangers, the charity and goodwill shown by pilgrims from north and south alike. There were so many whose presence left a lasting imprint upon my heart, and now, in this remembering, I am sincerely and humbly grateful to them all.

Memories flooded back then in sudden bursts of mindfulness, arriving not in sequence but as moments—whole and alive. That day's journey, a modest 16.7 kilometres, carried me toward **Cacabelos,** my destination by late afternoon. In Roman times, it served as an administrative centre for the gold mining operations that once fed the empire's ambitions in Hispania. For me, it would become something else entirely: a place of rest for a weary soul and torn feet. My lodging was simple, ranch-like in style, yet the front wall held a curious folk-art painting that immediately caught my attention. It depicted a young Jesus seated at a table, playing cards with Saint Anthony of Padua. The image unsettled and intrigued me in equal measure. Why cards, I wondered, between Master and servant? Chance and providence sharing the same table? I never discovered the artist's intention, but the images stayed with me long after.

Chapter 14. The End of a Trail.

Saint Anthony had been a soldier once, then a hero of faith. He left the Augustinian order to become a Franciscan monk. He went on to establish sixteen hospitals along the Camino to tend to those afflicted by a strange and terrible illness known in medieval times as *Saint Anthony's Fire*. He travelled to Africa to convert the Moors, returned unsuccessfully and largely ignored, and for a time lived in obscurity. Yet from that obscurity, he rose to become a professor of theology, teaching in Bologna, Toulouse, Montpellier, and Padua. Later, he gave up academia altogether to become a preacher and gifted orator, travelling throughout France, Spain, and Italy. Even in his own lifetime, he was regarded as legendary, reputed to work miracles, and known as the patron saint of lost souls and lost things.

Since childhood, it had been my habit to lean on his help. So it did not feel unusual—almost inevitable—that I should find refuge in a small albergue devoted to both Jesus and Saint Anthony. After a quick, nourishing meal in the kitchen, I retreated to my room and fell asleep almost the moment my head touched the pillow.

I had not bothered to lock the door or hide my money, phone, or possessions. I rested instead in the quiet trust of my childhood faith, believing myself watched over by Saint Anthony, protector and guide. That night at the Albergue de Mercadorio was exactly the pause I needed. Isolated and remote, Mercadorio was little more than a desert oasis: a solitary restaurant and an albergue standing watch over passing pilgrims. Yet in its simplicity, it offered me a rare and gentle peace.

The symbolism of the mural—the card game between Jesus and Saint Anthony—returned to me now with new clarity. It spoke of fate played against surrender, of chance set before trust. In that image, I recognised my own inner conflict. Along the Way, I had gained invaluable insight not only through visits to small country churches and vast cathedrals, but through a growing symbolic understanding of my relationship with God. Yet it was not only the sacred spaces that taught me. The albergues themselves—humble, chaotic, generous, or austere—had left their own indelible impressions, shaping meaning from the very beginning of the Camino.

My first night, high in a rooftop loft, gazing toward the Pyrenees as daylight faded, had been a quiet prophecy of what lay ahead—the long crossing of mountains, both outer and inner. The following night at Roncesvalles carried an even darker symbolism. Sleeping deep in the bowels of the monastery, in the basement, it felt like lying within the catacombs of my own emotional history—a burial of old understanding before any resurrection could occur.

As I looked back, I saw how each place I stayed had contributed to a deeper inward journey. There were nights on desert floors, on verandas, among animals in mountain villages, or packed into dormitories with seventy beds set four abreast. From a top bunk, every snore, groan, fart, or restless turning rippled through the night like a shared confession of human frailty—yet somehow, sleep still came, peaceful and restorative. Other nights were less forgiving: the roar of all-night parties raging like a wild bar at the edge of the world; the relentless scratching of a rat in the wall, determined to disturb any illusion of stillness. Or falling from a top bunk, I had the faint hope of being quiet as i made my way to the toilet. And then there were the rare five-star refuges I allowed myself perhaps once a week—the small luxury of a fresh bar of soap, a thick towel, and the privacy of a hot shower taken without interruption or impatience from those waiting outside, and some nights left me wondering why I had bothered to stop at all. Others filled me with quiet awe. Yet I regret none of them. Each stay, in its own imperfect way, carried symbolism and offered a lesson. Together they formed a living parable of the Camino itself: discomfort and grace, chaos and sanctuary, fate and surrender woven into the same unfolding path.

And so I came to understand that the Camino was never asking me to arrive with answers, only with honesty. Each bed, each village, each climb and descent was not a test to be passed, but an invitation to loosen my grip. What I once called faith in my youth had been certainty—clear lines, firm beliefs, a confidence that God could be named, defined, even bargained with. What I carried now was something quieter and far less specific: a willingness to walk without knowing.

In my younger years, I believed surrender meant loss. On this Way, I learned it meant release. Release of the need to control outcomes, to explain suffering, to justify the long ache of abandonment and desire. The Camino did not remove my pain; it taught me how to carry it lightly, and when the time came, how to set it down. Like the stones left at the Cruz Ferro, I began to see that surrender was not a single act, but a practice—repeated daily, sometimes hourly. It appeared in silence shared with strangers, in laughter that broke without warning, in nights of discomfort that somehow gave way to peace. It revealed itself not in visions or miracles, but in the steady rhythm of walking, step after step, breath after breath.

I no longer needed God to be proven to me. Presence was enough. The Way itself became the prayer.

And so I walk on—older now, less confident, yet more at peace. If I return again and again to these pages, to these memories, it is not to relive what was, but to remember how to let go. To remember that the sweetest surrender is not resignation, but trust: trust in the slow work of God, trust in the unfolding path, trust that even without clarity, the journey is still held.

An awakening is the gift the Camino left me with—not answers, but grace. Not certainty, but freedom. And in that freedom, a quiet, enduring peace.

I found myself looking back over the old website I had created in those days, rereading the advice I had written for fellow pilgrims. It felt like a message sent to me in the future—a timely reminder of how essential it is to be rightly prepared for the journey, both outwardly and within.

Consulting my notes and my website, I smiled at my own practical honesty. Although I had already jettisoned two kilos a week or two earlier, I was still carrying close to thirteen kilos and remained acutely aware of the excess weight. I resolved then to shed another three kilos before Santiago, posting unnecessary items home when I reached the next sizeable village with a post office. The Camino, I had learned, has little patience for what we carry out of fear rather than need.

The blisters had almost healed, yet my feet remained hot and swollen from the relentless pounding and the extremes of a Spanish summer. Still, the lessons of long-distance walking were settling into my bones. I had learned to wear only light, breathable clothing in the heat; to drink water steadily rather than desperately; to keep my energy up with simple, nourishing food; to slip into sandals whenever possible and let my feet breathe. Above all, I had learned the golden rule: carry no more than ten per cent of your body weight on your back.

I had written these words for others, but now I recognised them as guidance for myself. The Camino was teaching me, again and again, that suffering is often unnecessary, that simplicity is strength, and that wisdom—like lightening one's pack—comes from knowing what to let go of. As my load grew lighter, so too did something loosen in my spirit.

Surrender, I was learning, was not collapse or defeat, but discernment—the courage to choose what truly sustains and to let the rest fall away. The Camino was teaching me, step by step, that freedom is not found in adding strength, but in releasing weight, until walking itself becomes prayer.

I kept myself content by singing songs as I walked, shaping poems in rhythm with my steps, catching fragments of melody on the wind, and frequently stopping to cool my weary feet and update my journal. At the time, I had no idea that this daily practice of writing—scribbled thoughts, half-formed prayers, observations made in exhaustion or quiet joy—would one day become the backbone of a Camino book still waiting to be born. Back then, the journal was simply a companion, a way of emptying my mind so I could keep walking lightly.

I had crossed so many thresholds already—physical, emotional, and unseen—that the act of recording them felt less like documentation and more like release. Each entry was a laying down of weight, a pause between one breath and the next. Words arrived not as something I chased, but as something that met me on the road, much like the Camino itself. Looking back now, I can see that the path was shaping me twice over: once through the miles underfoot, and again through the quiet discipline of noticing, reflecting, and letting go. What I thought was merely passing time was, in truth, a slow act of surrender—one page at a time.

I had crossed the medieval **Ponte Aspera** bridge and the River **Celerio** on leaving Sarria, before beginning the steady climb toward **Alto de Páramo**—a demanding ascent made heavier by the heat of the day. From there, the Way led me through a shaded oak forest to the small hamlet of **Viler**, and onward to **Barbadelo**, a distance of some six kilometres that took me nearly two hours to complete. My pace had slowed, not from reluctance, but from a growing attentiveness to my body and the quiet counsel of fatigue.

Barbadelo had once been a thriving commercial centre, mentioned in the **Codex Calixtinus**, the twelfth-century manuscript traditionally attributed to Pope Callixtus II, though now widely believed to have been compiled and arranged by the French scholar **Aymeric Picaud,** and those days of prosperity had long since passed. What I found instead was a modest snack stand, a faint echo of its former importance. There, I purchased a bottle of water to supplement the two I had already filled at a fountain earlier on the Way. The stand offered simple provisions—fruit, mixed nuts, and a slab of dense stone cake—humble fare, yet sufficient to carry me through until the evening meal.

In that simplicity, Barbadelo revealed itself not as a place of loss, but of quiet sufficiency—another lesson from the Camino, teaching me once again that what is needed is rarely extravagant, and almost always enough.

As I ate, I became aware that the Camino itself was changing. The long, empty stretches of the Meseta were now far behind me. Villages appeared more frequently, paths converged, and unfamiliar faces were replaced by pilgrims I recognised from days before. The Way was narrowing—not just in distance, but in intention. Each step carried a subtle sense of gathering, as though all the wandering miles were quietly drawing themselves toward a single point.

Santiago was still days away, but it no longer felt distant. It was no longer an idea or a promise on the horizon; it had become a presence, felt rather than seen. And with that nearness came an unexpected realisation: the closer I came to the end, the less certain I felt about what, exactly, I was meant to arrive with—or leave behind.

Re-energised, I walked a further **12.7 kilometres** along a gentle downward slope, passing a succession of abandoned hamlets and small villages before arriving at **Mercadoiro**, another of those desert oases that appear just when one's resolve is being tested. I had already walked **16.9 kilometres** in the heat of the day, yet something had shifted within me. There was now a fire in my belly—a quiet but unmistakable determination—that urged me onward toward Santiago.

Along the way, I came upon a small gathering of stones, notes, and photographs piled near a Camino marker. On a nearby stone fence, a simple sign had been erected. It read:

"Lay down your sorrow." The words stopped me in my tracks.

The monument milestone was clearly a place of release for those who had not walked the entire length of the Camino and therefore had not laid down their burdens at the **Cruz de Ferro**, near Foncebadón. Many pilgrims were content to walk only the final **100 kilometres** to Santiago, carefully collecting stamps in their pilgrim passports at albergues, churches, and museums—just enough to qualify for the **Compostela** certificate upon arrival. Others believed the journey was not complete without continuing another **90 kilometres beyond** Santiago to **Finisterre**, the ancient "end of the world," where burdens were symbolically burned or cast into the sea. Stones, clothing, journals—whatever carried meaning—were surrendered to fire or water in a final act of release. As the saying goes, *Whatever floats your boat*. I did not judge any of it. Each pilgrim must walk their own Way. For my part, I had walked the full **800 kilometres**, and I knew I carried no desire to walk further once Santiago was reached. The letting go had already been happening—step by step, blister by blister, mile by mile. I had laid things down in silence, without ceremony, long before this marker appeared beside the path.

As I moved on, I came to understand something more clearly than before: surrender does not depend on distance, ritual, or proof. It comes when the soul is ready—whether at a cross on a windswept mountain, beside a stone fence on a quiet road, or simply in the willingness to keep walking without needing to carry everything to the end. And now, with Santiago drawing ever closer, I sensed that the final miles would ask not for more effort—but for less. Less striving. Less certainty. And a deeper trust in the quiet work already done.

As I approached those final days, the Camino no longer felt measured in kilometres but in quiet reckonings. I rose before dawn, stepping onto the Way at first light, gauging each village by the hollow in my stomach and the promise of coffee. These pauses became small liturgies—time to journal a line or two, to listen inwardly, then shoulder the pack again with a gentler resolve. By mid-afternoon, I would seek a church—cool stone, dim light—where silence pressed more deeply than prayer. There I sat, letting the road settle inside me, before finding an albergue, washing the dust from my skin, sharing a pilgrim's meal, and surrendering early to sleep. In dreams, faces returned: pilgrims met and parted, their stories braided into my own.

Walking had become mindfulness in motion. My stride even, my breath steady, I passed through abandoned hamlets and living villages alike—each a reminder of what endures and what fades. "Buen Camino" echoed constantly, offered and received, less greeting now than benediction.

The constant rhythm of my feet, the oasis of village kindness, the long stretches of silence—these had stripped away what was unnecessary. I recalled the sign once posted beside a stone wall: *"Lay down your sorrow."* Others had chosen where and how to do that—at Cruz de Ferro, at Finisterre, or within the final hundred kilometres. For me, the laying down was already happening, step by step. The closer I came to Santiago, the lighter the inner load felt, not because it was gone, but because I had learned how to carry it—and, at last, how to let it go.

Once again, my usual sense of distance failed me on that near-final morning. I set out through vineyards and cherry orchards, the Galician hills unfolding gently ahead, only to find myself, sooner than expected, a few kilometres short of Villafranca del Bierzo. It felt like a brief but beautiful oasis— a pause rather than a destination—before the longer pull toward La Faba, some thirty-four kilometres further on, my intended goal for the day. The Way climbed steadily from my overnight albergue. After many kilometres of ascent, I stopped at a small roadside albergue and wandered into its café bar for an early lunch.

Seated at the bar, my attention was unexpectedly drawn to a young blonde woman in a colourful floral dress and elegant sandals, deep in animated conversation with the barman in fluent Spanish. She was unmistakably not dressed as a pilgrim, yet she carried herself with ease and familiarity. When the barman stepped away to prepare my meal, she sat quietly, sipping local wine. At the same time, I found myself curiously intrigued by this fair-haired presence who moments earlier had been laughing easily in the local tongue.

When the tapas arrived—a generous plate placed between us—she turned and invited me, in a perfect Irish-American accent, to share her feast while I waited for my own order. She introduced herself as Marie and, almost immediately, began unfolding her story. I ordered an alcohol-free beer, enjoyed my Spanish pie, and accepted my share of her tapas as we moved to a table in the garden outside. It emerged that she had arrived by bus and stayed in the albergue opposite, taking time to shower and dress beautifully before lunch. I made a mental note—half amused, half practical—to remember that the albergue should stay the day longer than planned.

Marie was a New York restaurant owner whose life had been undone by floodwaters that swept through her neighbourhood a decade earlier. As she fought changing regulations to reopen, her father fell gravely ill and died, leaving her to carry both grief and responsibility alone. She spoke of him often, tears gathering each time, and it was clear to me that, like so many of us, she had come to the Camino to lay down burdens she could no longer hold. In her younger years, she had lived in South America, learning Spanish in a small village—hence her easy banter with the barman as more drinks were ordered and conversations drifted.

Our intimacy of exchange was interrupted by the arrival of three Irish women I had walked with earlier on the Way. I took the moment to check the albergue across the street, only to find it already full. The window had closed. I returned to the table, joined the Irish women once more, and though part of me hoped—perhaps foolishly—that a bed might somehow be shared, the day had other intentions. Instead, I sang them Irish songs, kissed each farewell with warmth and gratitude, and shouldered my pack once again.

As I walked on toward the next village, the light beginning to fade, I understood that this too was the Camino's lesson: encounters are gifts, not possessions. Some arrive dressed as pilgrims, others in flowers and sandals; some walk beside you for weeks, others for a single hour. Each leaves something behind. With hope still flickering and surrender now familiar, I walked on toward the next bed, the next silence, the road still teaching me how—and when—to let go.

Walking on toward the next village, I recognised the pattern clearly: the Camino introduces what you need at the moment you are ready to receive it—and removes it when you are not meant to stay. From the Pyrenees to Galicia, the faces had changed, but the lesson had deepened. I was learning to pace not just my body, but my heart; to carry fewer stories, fewer expectations, fewer hesitations.

Now, as I recall these moments in my diary, I see how each encounter—early and late—formed a single rhythm of hope and surrender. The Way was quietly preparing me for Santiago, not by adding meaning, but by teaching me when to let go and walk on.

Recalling the journey from **Sarria to Santiago** left many indelible marks upon my heart and soul. The procession of pretty villages, ancient oak trees offering shade to weary, thirsty travellers, Romanesque churches, and cobblestoned roads stirred something deep within me—a quiet remembrance of days long past and lives once lived with slower purpose.

The hamlets of **Barbadelo**, the steady hills rising toward the **Serra de Ligonde,** and the passage through the sleepy villages of **Gondar** and **Ventas de Narón** all blended into a single unfolding experience. Churches such as Santa María in Castromaior and Eirexe, with their statues of Daniel in the lions' den and saints standing gently among animals, seemed to breathe alongside the pilgrim, becoming companions rather than monuments.

Chapter 15. Strange Ways.

The trail continued downhill, past **Casanova**—steeped in legend, as the pilgrim's own mind often is—and onward to **Leboreiro**, before arriving at the lively markets of **Melide.** There, the taste of boiled octopus —pulpo a la gallega — served as a celebratory yet straightforward rite—one shared by countless pilgrims before me, grounding the sacred journey in the ordinary joy of food and fellowship.

Streams crossed our path, forest tracks enclosed us, and the villages of Boente and its church dedicated to Santiago offered solemn reminders of Saint James and of every pilgrim who had walked before—each one seeking to let go and let God, stepping out of darkness toward the light of a newly born day.

The remaining kilometres carried me through woods, more drowsy villages, and across yet more streams—each crossing a gentle reminder of another bridge passed, another road less travelled now behind me. Thoughts of the pilgrims I had walked with, laughed with, and even cried with began quietly settling into the corners of my memory, no longer companions on the road, but companions of the heart.

Eventually, I reached **Lavacolla,** on the outskirts of Santiago. It was here that pilgrims traditionally washed their feet in the river, a final act of cleansing before arrival. Rows of eucalyptus trees—so reminiscent of those from my homeland in Australia—lined the path onward to Monte do Gozo. And there, as generations of pilgrims had done before me, I caught my first glimpse of the cathedral spires rising in the distance: the long-sought Cathedral of Santiago, at once real and unreal, drawing the journey to its sacred threshold.

Here I was, walking the final five kilometres into the city, meeting again—here and there—pilgrims I had walked beside during the long weeks of the journey. Faces reappeared as if summoned by memory itself. As I look back now, I recognise how those emotional links return not as full portraits, but as fleeting presences. They were friends of the road, yet I knew only the facets of themselves they offered in passing.

I never saw their shadow selves. What I encountered instead was the child within—unburdened, playful, creative—rising above the darker layers to reveal something more genuine. Through shared pain and sorrow, laughter and silence, we glimpsed one another's authentic selves, briefly freed from the masks demanded by first-world life. Like me, they were casting off old cloaks: habits, roles, expectations that no longer served them.

In each pilgrim, I recognised a truth I had long suspected—we were square pegs, each of us, trying for much of our lives to fit into the round holes of the world. Pilgrims on an inner journey rarely fit into the places they are told they should. We walk differently. We listen differently. We feel more than is comfortable.

Now, in my later years, looking back on both my life's journey and The Way's journey, I can see with clearer vision what lay ahead even then. As I approached the Cathedral, I felt ready for a benediction of the soul. The great *botafumeiro* swinging through the nave, the Mass that followed—these were not endings, but mirrors of a more profound truth: that my journey, then as now, was an offering. A small act of sacrifice in the service of others, which in turn carries its own quiet reward.

I can still hear the priest's voice from that Cathedral homily: *"You have walked The Way—your pilgrimage—out of darkness into light. It is time now to let go of your burdens. Put down your pack. And live—really live."*

That lesson was not yet fully learned on my first Camino. Other lessons followed—of passion and shame, of guidance found through trial and error—on later Caminos, and on roads not marked by yellow arrows. Yet as I sit here now, I recognise this enduring truth: every day is a Camino.

It is good to look back and remember what mattered on The Way, but each new day offers another path to walk, another invitation to surrender. I hold what has passed with gratitude, and I remain attentive to what still asks to be lived. With that, I closed this diary, the first book I had revisited, and reached for another—ready to reconsider other journeys, both walked and yet to come.

Something was drawing me back to Santiago. I recalled crossing the bridge over the stream, leaving the dirt path I had been walking on, and thinking of the pilgrims of old. Near the village of Lavacolla, they took their final wash in the river before entering the city and the Cathedral. It struck me then that not all of them would have washed, and that the benediction awaiting them was as much a practical concern as a sacred one.

As pilgrims gathered for Mass, the stench of long journeys and unwashed bodies would have filled the nave—until it was overtaken by the sweet, heavy incense of the great *botafumeiro*, the famed "smoke belcher," swinging high above their heads. Perhaps this was part of the medieval Church's wisdom. At eighty kilograms and over a metre and a half tall, it required eight strong men to haul it on ropes, sending clouds of incense cascading over the congregation—sanctifying the air, disguising the smell, cleansing body and spirit alike. These days, when pilgrims arrive showered from albergues and hotels, the spectacle feels as theatrical as it is sacred. To my more cynical mind, it borders on ritualised drama. And yet, the moment still holds its power.

I was reminded too that Santiago was once a Roman city, later ruled by the Visigoths. Stories of spirits, ghosts, and witches linger in the folklore of Galicia, and they drifted through my thoughts as I considered the remains of St James beneath the Cathedral altar—remains before which countless pilgrims had knelt in hope, fear, gratitude, and doubt. Legend has it that his spirit was guarded by Templar knights who protected pilgrims along The Way in medieval times, and that St James himself —*Santiago Matamoros*—rode into battle on a white horse, flaming sword raised, leading Spanish troops against the Moors.

There is, of course, no historical record of such a battle. The timeline alone unravels the myth. St James was beheaded in Jerusalem by order of King Herod nearly eight hundred years before these stories emerged. Tradition claims his body and head were gathered by followers and set adrift, Viking-style, on a barge that carried him to the Galician coast. His remains were later "discovered" when a mysterious light appeared on a hillside, guiding a fisherman to the site. Whether this, too, is a myth is impossible to know. What is recorded is that a local bishop declared the remains to be those of **St James,** enshrined them in what would become Santiago, and in doing so gave rise to one of the greatest pilgrimages in Christendom. It is recorded in Christian scrolls that a small portion of his remains was scattered before the battle. Perhaps none of it happened at all. It is equally likely that St James never set foot in Spain, never rode a horse, never lifted a sword. And yet, I resolved to let the questions rest. Each time I entered the Cathedral on later Caminos, I still made my way to the burial chamber beneath the altar and prayed—just in case the myth held a more profound truth than history could verify.

Strange things do happen on the Camino. At least, they seem to. As written in the *Codex Calixtinus*:
"The most excellent city of the Apostle, complete with all its delights, having in its care the precious body of St James, is recognised as the luckiest and noblest city of all Spain."

Whether luck, legend, or longing drew me back, I could no longer tell. Perhaps it was to surrender itself, accepting that not everything must be proven to be meaningful.
I had been drawn to the city of kings—of Galicia and León—those who were crowned here in the Cathedral. Leon was once the capital of Galicia, a city fortified in the eleventh century after suffering Muslim incursions from Al-Andalus; a city of deep architectural wealth and enduring power, long regarded as the most important centre on the Galician Peninsula through the ages. This was the long-awaited city I finally encountered on my first Camino, entering Santiago on the 25th of August 2013, when I received my first **Compostela certificate,** having walked some eight hundred kilometres across northern Spain in the searing summer heat, along the same ancient path taken by pilgrims since medieval times.

Santiago was the city at the end of The Way walked by St Francis of Assisi and St Anthony of Portugal; by the Way of Charlemagne and his nephew Roland; by Napoleon, who marched his armies across northern Spain; and by the one who began it all—St James. And now it was also the Way of my newfound friends, my brothers and sisters of the Camino and me. I had imagined that some mythical sword of discernment awaited me here. Instead, I discovered that the pen was lighter than the sword, and yet far mightier. I was inspired not to conquer anything, but to write—to give voice to the journey itself. The book became my weapon, my offering, my way of letting go.

Even then, I would return to Santiago twice more, still carrying subtle illusions—that surrender might finally arrive through story, through song, through the next Camino. I was already conscious of the strong undercurrent of Celtic mysticism, witchcraft, and occult symbolism that continues to coexist with Christianity in Galicia. My guidebook even warned that, in the early dawn hours, the spirits of the night were said to linger on the city's outskirts. It is advised that, should one be confronted, a circle should be drawn on the ground and stepped into, and that no candle should ever be accepted from a stranger, for this was said to be the means by which a pilgrim might be drawn into a spell.

I had noticed stone crosses placed at crossroads along The Way, bearing mementoes, photographs, and tokens for pilgrims who had died. It crossed my mind—perhaps unfairly—that some may have perished through exhaustion alone, while others, in local imagination, were believed to linger as restless energies in the hills where they had once lived and breathed. The guidebook offered one final, almost playful remedy should all else fail: to drink *queimada*, the Galician fire-water—a potent spirit distilled from wine and infused with lemon peel, coffee beans, cinnamon, and sugar, then set alight while a spell is spoken to ward off evil spirits and witches alike.

By then, I no longer drank alcohol of any kind, let alone ancient concoctions. Ghost stories did not frighten me; I had spent long, solitary hours in the bush even as a child, and had encountered enough of the unseen to respect it without fearing it. I kept the circle idea in mind, my eyes alert for any pilgrim bearing a candle. The closest I came to anything uncanny was strange lights in the forest before sunrise—later dismissed as moonlight reflecting through branches in the half-dark.

As I entered the city, the **Cathedral spires** rose once more on the horizon. In the shifting light, the shadows cast by that grand structure held both darkness and illumination. When I stepped inside, the sweet, heavy incense struck me again—not merely as ritual, but as symbol: a cleansing not only of pilgrims, but of the world's accumulated darkness. I longed for a new light to enter me fully. Yet surrender came slowly—so slowly that, in hindsight, it was perhaps what kept drawing me back to the Camino.

The many stories I would later write, the essence of my reflections, were shaped by walking through the shadows of my own life: the mission of mountains, the written word as a means of release, the search for new horizons like an explorer on an inner expedition. Silence, mystery, detachment, fleeting moments, nature, ageing, and the gradual awakening into self-understanding all became companions on the path. And still, I had not fully unearthed my soul. I had not yet entirely surrendered to whatever it is that constitutes my ultimate divine plan.

That, too, was part of The Way.

I was drawn for the moment to a reference in the Bible Verse. Romans 12:2 - a key scripture telling believers not to conform to worldly patterns but to be transformed by the renewal of their minds, allowing them to discern God's good, acceptable, and perfect will, encouraging a spiritual transformation instead of worldly imitation. It emphasises changing one's thinking to align with God's perspective, moving away from temporary desires and towards a life reflecting divine purpose and values.

Still determined to return home with something symbolic to remember my Camino, I purchased a black T-shirt with the symbolic **sword of Santiago** on the front. I also had my **Compestella certificate,** but it was not enough. I demanded my letting go, so I opened my next diary entry to review and recall the next two Caminos I was to venture upon.

Chapter 16. Deception at Depth.

I had to turn once more to my daily reflections and noticed the current reading: "*Accepting Our Present Circumstances*." The words were written by Bill Wilson, co-founder of **Alcoholics Anonymous,** some seventy years earlier:

"Our very first problem is to accept our present circumstances as they are, ourselves as we are, and the people about us as they are. This is to adopt a realistic humility without which genuine advance can ever begin. Again and again, we shall need to return to that unflattering point of departure. Each Step is an exercise in acceptance that we can profitably practice every day of our lives.' Provided we strenuously avoid turning these realistic surveys of the facts of life into unrealistic alibis for apathy and defeatism, they can be the sure foundation upon which increased emotional health—and therefore spiritual progress—can be built."

The wisdom of these words settled deeply within me. Acceptance—of circumstance, of self, of the ever-changing tide of emotion—required discipline and clarity of thought. It was not passive resignation, but an active stance: standing honestly where I was, without embellishment or escape.

Once again, the lessons of past Caminos rose to the surface. I found myself imagining the **Cathedral in Santiago,** yet hesitated. To what avail, I wondered? The same sense of presence, the exact quiet alignment, could be found in a daily resolve, a simple act of service, attendance at a local church, or a solitary moment in stillness before my Maker—or whatever name I now gave to that presence.

And yet, the edge to walk another Camino persisted. So too did the longing to embrace new love, despite already having known it. That restless hunger—mistaken once again for destiny—drew me onward, this time to Portugal. There I embraced another lover, only to find lust, deception, and shame intruding upon my fragile sense of well-being. It was enough to undo me.

I returned to Australia carrying the familiar companions of depression and anxiety. And as had happened before, once the dust settled, my thoughts turned again to **The Way.** Another Camino called—this time not for romance or redemption, but for myself: for wellbeing, for simplicity, for the spirit of adventure that still stirred within me. Like an early explorer setting out toward an unseen frontier, I prepared to walk once more. But here I must pause. For I see now that I had always believed I needed a goal for my Caminos. At least, I thought I did—until now.

I see now that the need for a goal had quietly become another pack I carried on my back. For years, purpose had masqueraded as faith. Direction had stood in for trust. I believed that if I named the destination clearly enough—Santiago, Finisterre, love, healing, absolution—then meaning would reveal itself somewhere along the road. Yet the Camino, patient teacher that it is, had been whispering another truth all along: that surrender is not found at the end of the path, but in the willingness to walk without knowing why.

Each Camino I walked had been framed by intention. The first to survive. The second to redeem. The third was to repair what I thought was broken. And yet, beneath each noble aim, there lingered the same quiet fear—that without a reason, without a story to justify the journey, I might have to face myself as I was, unadorned and unrescued. This time, something had shifted.

As I sat with my diaries spread before me, the ink faded, and the pages softened with age, I realised that the Camino had never been about arriving at any holy place. Holiness had met me instead in blisters and boredom, in shared bread and borrowed silence, in moments of beauty that could not be planned and grief that could not be outrun. The road had given me companions for a season and then taken them away without explanation. It had taught me how to walk on, even when the heart lingered behind.

Letting go was the lesson that had taken years to mature: that surrender is not dramatic. It does not announce itself with incense and bells, nor does it always feel like relief. Often it feels like standing still when every instinct urges movement. Like laying down the pen when another chapter begs to be written. Like choosing presence over progress.

In my earlier Caminos, I had confused motion with growth. I had believed that walking farther meant going deeper. Now I was beginning to understand that depth sometimes asks us to stop—to listen rather than seek, to receive rather than strive. Sweet surrender, I was learning, was not the collapse of the will, but its quiet consent. Consent to this day as it is.To this body as it is. To this life—unfinished, unresolved, and still sacred.

The Camino had trained me well for this moment. Every morning departure before dawn, every farewell without promise of reunion, every time I had shouldered my pack not knowing where I would sleep that night—it had all been rehearsal, not for another journey across Spain or Portugal, but for the daily pilgrimage of living awake.

And so, as I closed that diary and reached for the next, I no longer asked where the road would take me. I wondered only whether I was willing to walk it honestly.

If I were to return to **The Way**—and I suspected I would—it would not be to find something missing, nor to lose myself in another story. It would be to give back what had been so freely given: presence, listening, kindness, and the hard-earned grace of one who knows that the path is never owned, only borrowed. For now, this Camino continued not beneath my feet, but within my days. And that, perhaps, was the truest surrender of all.

Still, I resolved to revisit the old diaries and the books I had written, to see whether something had gone astray in my present-day thinking—whether I had misunderstood the lessons about goals, about love as something to wash away regrets or cling to in the hope of being carried home in a healing embrace. And beneath it all, the quieter, more unsettling question lingered: where was God in all of this?

So I found myself recalling the unspoken mission of my last Camino, looking back across the first and second, and the well-worn paths of my own adventures—for better or worse, I could not yet say. What mattered was that I look honestly. Those three Caminos had awakened in me a wellspring of creative expression: poems, songs, and stories that had continued to surface long after my boots were put away. Since that first journey in 2013, I had walked The Way three times —the second in 2015 along the Portuguese route from Lisbon to Santiago, and the third in 2017 once more from St Jean to Santiago.

The first journey, as you, the reader, now appreciate, was profoundly cathartic. It loosened the grip of long-held circumstances that had trapped me and ushered me toward a renewed love of life through adventure. I began to step out from under the conditioning of my former self, letting go of tragic events, dispelling myths and legends that had haunted me since childhood. If nothing else, it led me toward a more realistic and compassionate understanding of the God of my own making.

The second journey, from **Lisbon to Santiago** in 2015, went deeper still. It stripped away further layers of belief and exposed hidden wounds I had unknowingly carried. Set against the pain of a toxic romance unfolding along that road, it offered hard-won insight. It planted in my soul a fragile but potent seed—the awakening power of imagination and inner truth. That Camino brought suffering and sorrow in equal measure, yet from it arose a renewed determination that would carry me into a third pilgrimage in 2017.

That **third Camino** proved both mythical and mystical—a time of quiet contemplation, of walking beside my own soul companion, and of learning what it meant to surrender to a power greater than myself. It completed a kind of trilogy, reintroducing me to the simple power of prayer and opening the path to my longest journey inward. Along that road, hidden treasures revealed themselves—not as answers neatly wrapped, but as glimpses of a more profound truth: that what we seek along The Way has always been waiting within us, patient and whole, asking only to be acknowledged.

As dawn lifted over the hilltop at **Long Reef,** the rocky coastline stretched out before me like a familiar threshold. The cool morning breeze and clear blue sky carried me back, effortlessly, to Spain and Portugal—to those first days beyond the Pyrenees when everything felt heightened and uncertain. Then, as now, I walked not to arrive anywhere in particular, but to listen. The waves rose and fell in their ancient rhythm, echoing the steady cadence of my footsteps, and I felt myself slip into that neutral space I had known since childhood— neither happy nor sad, simply present.

It was in such moments, both on the Camino and here on this shoreline, that I took stock of myself. In the Pyrenees, I had been intoxicated by the sheer sensuality of movement—the ache of muscles, the sharp mountain air, the novelty of new faces and fleeting connections. That same distraction had followed me years later on my Portuguese Camino, though in a subtler and more perilous form. What I mistook for companionship and affirmation was, in truth, a detour from the inward work I claimed to be undertaking.

I recalled the highs and lows of that second Camino, and in particular the aftermath of my involvement with a Portuguese medico I had met before leaving Australia. What began as anticipation became a whirlwind—Lisbon's allure, Porto's intensity, passion masquerading as purpose. I told myself her presence did not interfere with my pilgrimage. I insisted I had walked the Way before, that I knew myself well enough to indulge without consequence. Yet deep within, I knew better. What I had entered was not love, but a honeyed distraction— sweet, consuming, and ultimately empty.

The parallel with Peter's denial of Christ came to me unbidden. Three times the cock crowed, and three times Peter denied what he knew to be true. I, too, heard that crowing—

not as a sound, but as an inner reckoning—each time I denied that my spiritual focus had been compromised. When the passion faded, as it inevitably did, I was left exposed. The brief affirmation dissolved, and I found myself once again confronting depression and anxiety, returning to rehabilitation with a bruised spirit and a quieter heart.

Now, standing years later at Long Reef, contemplating another Camino, I understood something I had not grasped then. In the Pyrenees, I had learned endurance. On the Portuguese Way, I learned humility. Both taught me that goals, while helpful, can also obscure the more profound lesson if pursued without awareness. I had always resisted simple surrender, preferring to define my journey by milestones rather than moments. Yet suffering, I was reminded, belongs only to the day it is carried—and need not be rehearsed or prolonged.

It was here, on this very beach years earlier, that a piece of mahogany driftwood had caught my eye, rising and falling with the waves. That discovery had seeded another quest— one layered atop the spiritual journey I claimed to prioritise. The imagined wreck of a Portuguese caravella, lost to the vast seas between Africa and Australia, became a symbol of unfinished business, of history calling me outward rather than inward. I followed that call to Portugal, searching museums and records, hoping to anchor meaning in discovery. But the ship never revealed itself. Instead, what surfaced was grief, disillusionment, and the quiet recognition of my own misplaced longing.

Only later, at **Finisterre**, did another piece of mahogany driftwood appear—weathered, anonymous, unclaimed by history. It asked nothing of me. It simply was. And in that simplicity lay the lesson I now carry forward: the Camino does not reward haste, nor distraction, nor the layering of missions upon missions. It teaches pacing—of body, of heart, of thought. It invites reflection not to judge the past, but to integrate it.

So now, as I return to my diaries, my notes, my half-forgotten reflections, I do so with gentler eyes. Not to correct them, but to understand them. Not to seek another outward sign, but to recognise that God—quiet, patient, unassuming—had been present all along, waiting not at the destination, but in the spaces between each step.

So once more, my mind was drawn to Long Reef at sunrise, where I walked the familiar shoreline as the tide breathed in and out like a patient teacher, carrying me back to Spain and Portugal and to the many Caminos already etched into my body and soul. The weight I had then was not in my pack but within desires, dreams, romances, myths, and goals I believed necessary to give the journey meaning. Yet each time I tried to outrun that weight with passion, purpose, or pursuit, it returned heavier, like a stone tied to the heart. Lust disguised itself as love, ambition as calling, and legend as truth, until surrender became unavoidable.

Along the Way, signs appeared not as answers but as invitations: driftwood shaped by distant wrecks, incense rising to cleanse more than bodies, ancient myths that dissolved under honest prayer, and a simple wooden crucifix half-buried in the sand, reminding me that direction does not come from striving but from stillness. The Camino, like the sea, taught me that progress is not measured by how far we walk, nor by what we seek, but by what we are finally willing to lay down. In releasing the need for outcomes, explanations, or even enlightenment itself, I discovered that the true pilgrimage was an unburdening. On this inward descent, the soul, lightened at last, learns to trust the rhythm of grace and to walk, not toward something, but within it.

The Camino Diaries may now and then be taken out of storage and look up once more as a rear-view mirror to recall not just places and faces but the emotions and inner movements bound to them. They hold the full weight of what was lived—the outward act of walking becomes a vessel for inward transformation, where distance, terrain, and fatigue strip away illusion and expose unresolved wounds, borrowed identities, and deeper longings. The Pyrenees climbed in heat and rain, the albergues, Cruz de Ferro, and Finisterre were never merely destinations but symbols of a repeated discipline of letting go, lessons preserved not as relics of achievement but as offerings for those who may one day walk their own narrow road toward spiritual sanity. Desire, romance, and sensual distraction revealed how easily attention drifts from inner work to external validation, until honesty and presence gently reclaim it.

Santiago was honest, the certificates authentic, yet they testify only that the road was walked, not that the work was finished. True faith emerged not from doctrine but from suffering, doubt, prayer, silence, and living encounters with fellow pilgrims; pain became instruction rather than punishment, a doorway rather than an end. Through poetry, journaling, songs, and stories, raw experience was transmuted into wisdom, and the **three Caminos** revealed themselves not as failures or conclusions but as a single path endlessly re-walked at deeper levels.

Some treasures have been spoken, others remain quietly held, but all point to the same truth: transformation is unfinished, surrender is ongoing, and acceptance—yours and mine—is the key that unlocks consciousness in the fleeting now. Whether another Camino awaits is not mine to decide; that, as ever, rests in hands greater than my own.

Chapter 17. Epilogue.

New Year's Day, 2026

As a final gesture in the Camino Diaries, I turn now to a blank page and a new year. In reflecting on what has unfolded through my Caminos and the events that followed in my life, I recognise that I stand at a quiet threshold—where the rush of the past gives way to the gentler flow of the present. The striving, the seeking, the relentless need to arrive somewhere else has softened. What remains is a growing attentiveness to where I already am. My future, as it now presents itself, is less about acquisition and far more about appreciation; less about ambition and more about presence. It is a season of learning how to be, rather than how to become.

There is a serenity beginning to take root that once would have unsettled me. The anxious urgency of youth—its need to prove, to conquer, to outrun fear—has loosened its grip. Life's storms, though not absent, have passed through me often enough that I no longer mistake turbulence for failure. In their wake lies a calmer sea, one in which I can finally steer my own course, liberated from professional constraint and the false obligations I once carried as duty. Mornings now arrive without haste. Time stretches, not as emptiness, but as invitation—an open field for reflection, reading, writing, walking, and simply watching the world move at its own pace.

Silence has become an ally rather than something to escape. It is not a void, but a richly textured space where memory, gratitude, and grief coexist without demand. In these quiet hours, I engage in an honest life review, tracing the long arc of my experiences and allowing both joy and sorrow to speak. Losses—of people, roles, dreams, versions of myself—are no longer resisted but gently acknowledged. This reconciliation with what has been and what cannot be recovered brings with it a settled acceptance, a deep interior peace that no longer depends on external validation.

What has emerged is a fundamental shift from doing to being, from accumulation to connection. The priorities that once seemed secondary now stand clearly in the foreground: maintaining health so that independence remains possible; cultivating purpose through contribution rather than achievement; and, above all, nurturing relationships. Legacy is no longer an abstract concern deferred to some imagined future. It lives here and now—in shared laughter with children and grandchildren, in the quiet passing on of hard-won wisdom, in the enduring bonds of family and friendship. If anything of my writing, songs, or stories endures, it will be because they were rooted in love rather than ego.

These octogenarian years, far from being a closing chapter, reveal themselves as a valuable season of integration—where reflection deepens connection and each day is lived with dignity and gratitude. Yet beneath this gentler rhythm, the fire that has carried me since boyhood still burns. I recognise it now not as restlessness, but as vitality. From the daring days of youth, through devotion to duty, risk, adventure, pain, failure, and surrender, that same spirit has endured. I am older, yes—but not finished. I still feel the call to dare, to risk, to affirm that I am alive.

The difference now lies in the direction of that energy. The thrill of the chase has given way to the courage of presence. What excites me is not conquest but availability—being there for those who suffer along this narrow road of life, despite my own limitations. It is still a learning, still a discipline: courage expressed through steadiness, determination tempered by discernment. I may move more slowly, but the will remains intact. As long as it does, I will continue.

I am not ready for contempt disguised as wisdom, nor resignation mistaken for surrender. True surrender, I have learned, is not withdrawal from life but deeper engagement with it—accepting each day as it arrives, acting for the greater good where I can, and refusing the excuses that masquerade as prudence. Such a Way, too, is a Camino: unfinished, ongoing, and quietly sacred.

And so, with gratitude for the road already walked and openness to whatever remains, I step into this new year—not in search of another destination, but grounded in the simple grace of being present on The Way.

Doug McPhillips, poet, singer, songwriter, and author, commenced his journey of discovery over a decade ago after life-changing experiences. The many tracks he has traversed through the Northern Hemisphere and down under in Australia and New Zealand have resulted in the facts and fiction of this novel.

Doug has recorded and sung songs related to this work, featuring a unique melody in the true Australian style. Doug has written many novels, an autobiography, two books of poetry, a travel guide and this book of inspirational guidance. He has also co-produced and recorded three albums of his songs.

Doug divides his time between work, family, friends, and those who seek guidance in following their heart's desires.

Ingram Spark Publishers
1 La Verge TN37086
Nashville Tennessee.

Printed in Australia
Lightning Source
76 Discovery Road South
Scoresby, Victoria 3179

21/1/26